Money Mafia

Jibril Williams

**Lock Down Publications and Ca$h
Presents**
Money Mafia
A Novel by *Jibril Williams*

2

Money Mafia

Lock Down Publications
P.O. Box 944
Stockbridge, Ga 30281
www.lockdownpublications.com

Copyright 2021 by Jibril Williams
Money Mafia

First October 2021
Printed in the United States of America

This is a work of fiction. Names, characters, places, and incidents either are products of the author's imagination or are used fictitiously. Any similarity to actual events or locales or persons, living or dead, is entirely coincidental.

Lock Down Publications
Like our page on Facebook: Lock Down Publications @
www.facebook.com/lockdownpublications.ldp

Book interior design by: **Shawn Walker**
Edited by: **Lashonda Johnson**

Jibril Williams

Stay Connected with Us!

Text **LOCKDOWN** to 22828 to stay up-to-date with new releases, sneak peaks, contests and more…

Thank you!

Submission Guideline.

Submit the first three chapters of your completed manuscript to ldpsubmissions@gmail.com, subject line: Your book's title. The manuscript must be in a .doc file and sent as an attachment. Document should be in Times New Roman, double spaced and in size 12 font. Also, provide your synopsis and full contact information. If sending multiple submissions, they must each be in a separate email.

Have a story but no way to send it electronically? You can still submit to LDP/Ca$h Presents. Send in the first three chapters, written or typed, of your completed manuscript to:

LDP: Submissions Dept
P.O. Box 944
Stockbridge, Ga 30281

DO NOT send original manuscript. Must be a duplicate.

Provide your synopsis and a cover letter containing your full contact information.

Thanks for considering LDP and Ca$h Presents.

Jibril Williams

Chapter 1

Slurp! Slurp! Slurp!

"You like that, Zaddi?"

Shoota's toes cracked and popped in his Louis Vuitton sneakers caused by the amazing fellatio he was experiencing tucked away behind the wheel of his AMG Benz Wagon. Shoota's only reply to the woman's question was to push her head back down on his pipe as she slowly licked the length on his nine inches causing him to palpitate in her hand.

She let a glob of spit dribble over her full lips onto Shoota's helmet. She worked the saliva over his wood before snaking him into the back of her throat. Shoota caught all the action on his iPhone that he held in his hand. Jassii never took her eyes off Shoota's phone. She was in a trance and he could tell that the true hoe was coming outta her.

Jassii slurped Shoota's dick viciously, every time Shoota's helmet hit her throat forcefully she gagged and her eyes watered. Jassii had one ridiculously long tongue like the porn star Cakey, and she was deadly with it. She wrapped her tongue around Shoota's beef log, like a snake would wrap itself around a tree branch. All suction with her lips and going up and down on Shoota pipe from the head of his base in a fluent motion with no hands. Shoota's rod was heavenly coated with Jassii mouth juices. He was in heaven. Shoota wanted to close his eyes and really enjoy the head he was receiving, but he couldn't afford to miss the action taking place in his lap.

Jassii acted like she was making love to the camera by the way she was looked in it. Shoota had to confess though Jassii looked sexy as fuck with his dick in her mouth.

I might download the footage on IG, Pornhub or some shit, he thought.

He didn't give a fuck whose bitch she was supposed to be. Best-selling Authors *Cash* and *NeNe Capri* wrote about trusting no bitch and that was key in the life he was living.

Jassii had been creeping around with Shoota for months now. Jassii claimed to be a full-blown lesbian, but it was obvious she wasn't because she was in Shoota's G-Wagon with a yard of dick in her mouth. Jassii was indeed a lesbian, but she had an itch for some real live, hard dick once in a while and Shoota was her Hydrocortisone cream to cure her itch.

Jassii normally didn't allow her hidden desires for a stiff one to go over one or two encounters, but Shoota's pipe game was *boss,* his swag was serious and it didn't hurt that he had an unlimited bag. So, she entertained him longer than she normally would have any other dick. Jassii was hesitant when she first started creeping around for the D because she been into lesbian relationships for six years. Her standing current relationship had been going on for the past two years. She really loved her girlfriend, but her girlfriend couldn't give her what Shoota could and that was real dick.

Dildos and strap-ons were cool, but they weren't like a real one no matter how real life they made them. Jassi learned from past relationships with men that they wasn't shit and they played mad games with females hearts and minds. Shoota had her second guessing her sexuality and thinking about crossing back over to strictly dickly but she was hesitant.

Jassii worked her lips, jaw and tongue like a true head scientist. She felt the hot splash of Shoota's semen spray inside her mouth. She didn't stop there, Jassii kept her suction going until she relieved Shoota of all his babies. She swished his man juices around in her mouth before she displayed them on her tongue for the camera to see.

"Hummm yummy!" Jassii said seductively after swallowing the dick cream and giggled into the camera.

Shoota turned the camera off and checked his Audemars Piguet. Shoota had about a half an hour before he had to make it to his meeting.

"Come on, Shoota, I see you are still hard. Come beat my guts up real quick," Jassii said, kicking off her Red Bottoms and unbuckling her white Balmain jeans, she shimmied out of them.

She wanted badly to fuck Shoota all over the new G-Wagon seats. It was something about the smell of fresh foreign leathers that made her pussy stupidly wet. Right then and there Jassii was slippery while wet.

"Naw, shawty hold fast. I got moves to make. I'll get with you on that," Shoota stated pulling his Louie V jeans back over his hips, securing his manhood in place and fastening his Louie V belt.

"Shoota, fuck that! I need to get me a shot of dick. I'm fiending like fuck!" Jassii said with an attitude.

She reached over for Shoota's belt buckle to free his rod, but he pushed her hand away and scanned the parking lot of Stadium Strip Club.

"You really gonna do a bitch like this, Shoota?" Jassii pouted, fastening her jeans back.

She angrily fumbled around on the truck's floor to locate her Red Bottoms and place them back on her size seven feet. She was heated.

Shoota ignored her temper tantrum. He removed the half smoked backwood from behind his ear and blazed it.

"So, you came down here just so I could suck you off in your new truck?" Jassii continued pouting.

Shoota couldn't stunt Jassii wasn't to be taken lightly in the looks department. Jassii had the type of body all walks of mankind worshipped, a flat stomach, a small waist, standing five foot three with hazel green eyes and a baby hippopotamus ass that kept the Stadium Strip Club packed with occupants geekin' to get a glimpse of the one and only Jas. When she was on stage performing naked, body covered in oil and tattoos men and women covered her body with money complimenting her beauty and sexiness. Jassii favored Fendi Red but was two shades darker.

"I told your spoiled ass I had something for ya with your fake no meat eating ass. You was so caught up thinking I was offering you the dick that you jumped on it soon as a nigga put the truck in park," Shoota spoke with a chuckle as he hit the backwood.

The potent scent made Jassii want to ask for a hit, but she knew from past experiences that Shoota wouldn't dare smoke behind her.

"I got this for you," Shoota said, reaching in the back of the G-Wagon and removing a blue and white Christian Dior bag. It was one of the designer's newest edition and Jassii knew the bag ran Shoota ten stacks easily.

Shoota set the bag in Jassii's lap, and Jassii's assumption was correct about the bag hitting Shoota's pocket, the price tag on the bag read $9, 436. Jassii loved everything designer that came with a hefty price tag.

"Thanks, Zaddi, let me properly thank you real quick with some supa wet-wet?" Jassii said, trying again to breach her throbbing walls in between her thighs.

She reached for Shoota's belt buckle, which she was again denied access.

"I told ya thirsty ass, I have moves to make. I'll fuck with you later on that shit," Shoota retorted.

"Fuck it!" Jassii said slightly offended from being rejected for the second time tonight. "I got to get ready to secure this bag anyway," Jassii mumbled as she opened the truck door and got out.

She stood on the outside of Shoota's truck with the door held open and her new bag in her hand. Clearly, she had an upset expression on her face because she wasn't able to get her kitty scratch. "When can I see you again?" Jassii asked before closing the door.

"I'll fuck with you in a few days," Shoota stated without looking at Jassii.

Jassii didn't like Shoota's response. She wondered how she'd lost control. She was the one that used to set the time and place when it came to creeping for the D, but now she was beggin' for the appointments.

"Psss!" Jassii sucked her teeth closing Shoota's truck door and strutted towards the Stadium Strip Club.

Shoota shook his head at the way Jassii's ass jiggled in her white Balmain jeans. He wanted to slay Jassii's little thick ass, but he had other plans for her cute ass.

***

Pushing his left foot down on the clutch and popping the Porsche Taycan into third gear, Musa gave the foreign engine some gas by pressing his right foot down on the accelerator making the Porsche lurch forward. The midnight blue Porsche cabin was somewhat tight, but it was beautiful designed and executed and snugly fitted with nary rattle or squeak. The 750 horsepower and 774lb from two motors powering all four wheels was eating the road up as Musa gripped the wheel tightly. He bopped his head back and forth to *Lil Baby & 42 Dugg Track, We Paid* the baseline bleed through his L7s subwoofers.

A cotton candy pink 911 Porsche spinning on black rims was beating up the road next to him. Musa popped the clutch and Taycan was slipped into fourth and adding some pressure on the car accelerator. The Taycan dugged into the road firmer and pulled away from the 911 effortlessly. The traffic was light but the few cars that occupied Suitland Parkway was a blur. It was as if the cars were sitting still as he and the 911 rocketed pass them. Feeling the 774 horsepower in the Taycan gave Musa an adrenaline rush. The speedometer on the dash was reading 135mph and it still had room to push the Porsche even faster.

Musa hit the cigarillo that hung from the corner of his chocolate lips. The smoke seeped from his nose. He eased off the gas a little because the 911 was becoming a small pink dot in his review. He eased to the right side of the parkway and caught his exit. Musa came off his exit, straightened up coming out the exit curve and hit it. Three minutes later, he turned the Taycan into the parking lot of an industrial warehouse where he kept merch from flat screens to laptops and electronics you could think of was stored here. This was one of Musa's businesses that he laundered the Mafia's illegal money through.

The warehouse, also better known as The Hub, was where the Money Mafia conducted their monthly mandatory meeting. Musa parked behind the warehouse along with the other foreign cars. Musa hopped out the Taycan and rested on its hood. He took a long drag of the cigarillo before plucking the end of it on the ground. He let out a huge cloud of smoke as the Pink 911 zipped behind The Hub. Musa smiled hard, showing off his pearly whites and a front tooth that bared a chip.

Musa threw his arms up in the air. "I told ya the Porsche Taycan is faster than the Porsche 911.

The Porsche 911 door opened and the baddest chick ever to push a 911 stepped out. Her four-inch pink Giuseppe Zanetti stilettos touched the pavement gracefully adding inches to Ace's 4'11 frame. Ace had an ass on her that many women went to see Dr. Miami to obtain, but hers was all natural, passed down from the essence of her mother. Ace was mixed with Jamaican and Guamanian. She had captivating gray eyes, the kind that men got lost in no matter the circumstances. Her C-cups sat healthy and ripe on her pecan-brown skinned chest. The form fitting Chanel revealed her ever luscious curves.

Once she emerged from the 911, the mohawk she rocked made her look like JT the rapper from City Girls. Ace was a girly girl, she was Money Mafia's first lady, and nothing to fuck off with.

"Okay, the Porsche Taycan is running harder than a run-a-way slave." Ace walked over to Musa and tossed him a stack of bills with a red rubber band around it. A small bet that they had placed on whose Porsche was the faster. "You gonna make a bitch go cop that Tesla," Ace boasted

"Go get it! And I would run that bitch in the ground and take your money!" Musa said excitedly.

"I would like to see that! But let's go in here and get this meeting under way. I see we are the last ones to get here." Ace scanned the cars in the parking lot, she recognized all the cars except for the black-on-black G-Wagon.

"It's crazy how we got two of the fastest cars out here but we are the last two getting to our meeting," Musa stated

"Well, that's one of the perks of being bosses!" Ace said tugging the hem of her Chanel dress and pulling it down over her thighs before she walked into The Hub.

Chapter 2

When Musa entered The Hub, he threw his arms in the air and administered some sarcasm. "It's about time you niggas showed up!"

The room was full of Money Mafia's most trusted members. The group stop conversing with one another and acknowledged their boss.

"Nigga, I hear ya talking shit! You're the one late as fuck," Brim stated walking up to Musa showing him some brotherly love with a dap and a shoulder hug. "What's up, fool?" Brim said, releasing Musa.

"You know what it is, Money Mafia all day," Musa capped.

"Ain't no other way," Brim retorted.

Brim was Money Mafia's youngest member. He'd been part of the organization since the beginning, and he was loyal to Musa. Brim was Money Mafia's livewire. His role in the organization was to lead all of Money Mafia's goons when niggas grew nuts the size of grapefruits, went against the grain and tried to put a stop to Money Mafia's cash flow. The work he did for and with his team had him eating good. Shit they all were, and Money Mafia was flaunting it like they were the next BMF. The Balmain sweats he wore testified that he was ruffing with money, that was an understatement though because the diamond Patek and diamond chain around his neck and the iced out doubled MMs spoked.

"I am money!" Brim was the short, stocky type. He stood a little over 5'5 with a menacing grin that always made inauthentic niggas perplexed when he was in their presence. The coldness in his brown eyes was a hint that Brim was slightly off his rocker. Old war marks tatted the goon's face. The ladies found his marks attractive right along with his swag and aggressiveness.

Musa walked around the room and dapped his team. Ace went straight to the bar, fixed her a drink and checked her phone to see if her love had checked in with her yet. Ace watched the body language of the most trusted. Her and Shoota's eyes met, and an unsettling exchange took place between them. Ace took a sip from her glass and watched Shoota over the glass rim. Only when Musa approached Shoota for a pound that's when he broke eye contact with her. Ace put it on her to do list to pull up on Shoota and check the temperature between them.

Shoota had been acting strange as fuck. The Henny burned Ace's throat as it went down. Ace was thinking that Shoota was back on the bullshit again. Every few months Shoota would get on the lame ass shit of trying to fuck her. It always ended with her denying Shoota access to the treasure between her legs. Musa, Brim and Shoota were like brothers to her but that never stopped Shoota from trying to crack open her candy jar.

Ace shook her head at Shoota's doggish way. It was niggas like Shoota that influenced her to be a lesbian. Ace was definitely gonna have a serious talk with Shoota.

Musa waved everyone over to stand around the custom pool table that homed two Ms in the table's middle. Ace took post next to Musa. Eight bodies stood around the table but their was only four members that were the core of Money Mafia. Brim, Shoota, Ace, and Musa was the brains.

Musa licked his full lips before he spoke, "I know we been waiting on this power move for a while now. The only reason I've been having the move on pause is because I wanted to make sure we had our position here in the city secured. Money Mafia is eating better than projects kids eating off an unlimited E.B.T card."

Laughter erupted around the pool table at Musa's analyst. Shoota knew where Musa's speech was leading and he was getting excited just thinking about how his status was going to change.

"The Money Mafia gonna expand in the next thirty days. We're gonna establish a few traps in the Capitol, District Heights and Springfield Maryland. Jus-Blaze, you wanted Capitol Heights, you got it. Shark Head, you on post out in District Heights and Stink, you're gonna man the Silver Spring traps. So, I hope you all got your teams ready. We're doing everything with finesse. Move light and give the locals a chance to eat with us. If niggas don't like the approach, then Money Mafia will shut down the traps and turn the heat up until them niggas get on board," Musa said, staring in the eyes of his most trusted.

All acknowledged and nodded their heads in agreement except Shoota and Brim. Fire burned in Shoota's eyes, Brim was a little disappointed. He knew Musa always had a reason for doing shit, so with Musa not giving him the opportunity to expand he held his tongue.

"I will be meeting individually with those who are expanding. Any questions?" Musa asked.

It was like Shoota was waiting for Musa to ask that question, because Shoota blurted his question out, "What the fuck happen to my request to expand to Baltimore?" The aggression in Shoota's voice didn't go unnoticed.

Musa looked at his childhood friend with a look of sternness.

"You requested and at this time your request is denied."

"But why?" Shoota asked, leaning on the edge of the pool table with a mug on his face.

Musa didn't like to be questioned in front of the Mafia, especially the way Shoota was doing. "The only reason why I'm gonna answer your question and tolerate your light disrespect is because you my day one and we done ate crumbs off the same plate. B-More isn't a city you can just walk in and start taking over. That city is heartless and unforgiving. Baltimore is one of them cities you have to be invited into by someone that's already establish and not by some broke nigga looking for a quick come up."

"But my people that cut B-more is solid and TTG all day," Shoota pleaded.

"And with all that being said you still don't know them B-More niggas well enough to open up shop in their city!" Musa raised his voice he was becoming irritated with Shoota. "I'm not saying no, I'm just saying not right now. B-more is forty-five minutes away from D.C. that's a long way from home if shit goes sour in Baltimore. Springfield, Capitol Heights, and District Heights is just across the D.C. line. It's easier access to them location," Musa tried to make it make sense to Shoota.

Shoota wasn't tryin' to hear none of that bullshit. He'd helped build Money Mafia from the ground up. How the fuck the late comers have a chance to advance while he'd been there since the beginning. In Shoota's mind that was unacceptable.

Ace watched the fuel in Shoota's eyes, she could tell Musa, and him was about to have a big blow out over this. She slightly shook her head in disgust.

"Are you good, Shoota?" Musa asked.

Shoota hesitated before he answered, "Yeah, for now!" He replied.

Musa was about to check the statement, but Ace bumped his arm with her elbow, indicating for Musa to let it go.

"Any more questions, comments or concerns?" Musa asked, letting his eyes survey the group.

Everyone shook their heads.

"I have a situation that needs to be addressed," Ace said, getting everyone's attention. She was nervous as fuck she didn't want to look weak in the eyes of her peers.

"What's going on, Ace!" Musa sensed Ace's reluctance.

"I fronted my lady's brother two bricks and now this nigga is ghosting me."

Creases formed in Musa and Brim's forehead. Shoota looked at her like she was the weakest bitch ever.

"How long ago was this?" Musa questioned Ace.

"About four months ago!"

What Musa heard angered him. "Give Shoota all the info on the nigga and he'll handle it," Musa stated.

"Man, fuck nawl. Why the fuck can't she handle her own shit. You got her as Capo of Money Mafia, and she can't even collect the money back from the work she fronted to some low life ass nigga?" Shoota spazzed, nostrils flaring like a raging bull.

He was tired of catering to Ace, and he wasn't feeling how she was running around the city like she was some type of trap queen.

"Nigga, I can handle my own situations. I been putting niggas in graves—" Ace couldn't finish her sentence before Musa leaped on top of the pool table that separated him and Shoota.

16

He quickly closed the gap between them. Musa was now in Shoota's face. They were standing nose to nose.

"My nigga, this is twice in one night that you questioned me in front of the fam about the decisions I make for this family." Spit from Musa's mouth sprinkled Shoota's face.

Feeling Musa's spit droplets hit his face, angered him even more, but a fight with Musa he didn't want. He was going to give Musa the satisfaction of backing out his face an inch.

"I'm not questioning you, my nigga, like you think. I'm just tryna get a better understanding of where I stand in this organization." Shoota spoke through clenched teeth.

"You not acting like it, Slim. You acting like you got some animosity in your heart with all that aggression you displaying toward family," said Musa.

Shoota never broke eye contact with his day one. Deep down he was crushed that Musa was in his grill like he was going to bring him harm. He felt Musa was trying to bitch him in front of Money Mafia, and he was doing it over a weak bitch.

"Naw, Musa, no animosity here. It's all love, fam," Shoota stated, backing away from him. Every member of Money Mafia's eyes were on them. Shoota threw the double M up in the air with his fingers and announced, "Money Mafia!"

"All day! Every day!" The room erupted in unison.

Shoota spun on his heels and exit The Hub.

Musa leaned against the pool table watching the back of Shoota as he left, wondering if Shoota's actions were the breeding of jealousy and envy, the type of cancer that destroyed so many families.

If so, he thought, what will it take to eradicate that type of cancer out of Money Mafia's ranks?

He couldn't phantom the thought of killing Shoota. He quickly tucked that idea away.

"Aye, Brim, get with Ace and handle that little problem she's having," Musa instructed.

Even though Brim felt like Shoota did about Ace, he was loyal to Musa. He would not openly voice how he felt. So, he just nodded his head and mouthed the words, "Say less."

Jibril Williams

Chapter 3

Lil Baby's vocals from his song *Social Distancing* bumped through Shoota's subwoofers at a low level. Soon as Shoota left The Hub. He twisted a fat cigarillo of white widow and mashed out in his Benz truck. His head felt like it weighed a ton in his chest, his mind was in a fog. Musa's actions at the meeting had him thinking some crazy ass shit about Musa and Ace. He couldn't understand how Musa selected Ace to be Money Mafia's Capo.

Ace hasn't done half the shit I've done for Musa or Money Mafia, Shoota thought as he pulled hard on the cigarillo.

The exotic seemed to put him in a greater fog, making him abhor the idea even further that Ace was his second boss. The sacrifice he made for Musa should have automatically given him a higher position in Money Mafia. Shoota's mind easily faded back to the day he made the ultimate sacrifice.

***

"Wassup Champ!" Musa hollered at Shoota from the driver's seat of his Chrysler.

Shoota stood in front of the buildings around Ledroit Park. Where he was selling nickel bags or rocks to the smokers that came through the projects. This was a trap they'd claimed as theirs since Musa mysteriously came across five kilos of some hard white.

"You know me, Mu, it's Money Mafia all day, every day!" Shoota shouted from the stoop he was standing on.

"Come take a ride with me, slim!" Musa yelled from his car.

Shoota threw up a finger and grabbed the zip lock bag full of nickel rocks out of the mailbox they were stashed in and took the work to Cookie's apartment. Cookie was a female that lived in the building who he was smashing. He stashed products and guns at her apartment, in return he kept her nails and hair done. He also kept her laced with hard dick. Shoota jogged back to Musa's waiting Chrysler 300.

"What's up, my nigga?" Shoota said once he got in the car and dapped Musa.

"Shit, a slight money move," Musa announced pulling away from the Ledroit Park buildings.

"Where are we headed?" Shoota asked pulling out a dime bag of loud pack and started twisting it up in a backwood.

"We about to slide through 7th and Taylor Street. I got the nigga Fat Corey wanting a double up. So, I'm gonna hit him off."

"Man, you gonna fuck with that crudie ass nigga. Man, turn around and let me grab the trey-five-seven." Shoota expressed.

"We good, Shoota, I got the highpoint 380 on me," Musa stated pulling the burner from between his thighs, showing Shoota.

"Give me the gun, I'll hold you down," Shoota protested.

"I got it with ya trigga happy ass! You always want to pop something," Musa chastise Shoota.

"I just don't trust Fat Corey grimy ass. You know how the nigga gets down and how he be rockin'," Shoota said seriously, passing Musa the backwood.

Musa and Shoota were childhood friends. They'd met in a homeless shelter for women. That was located on 14th and Park Raod NW. That's where the two grew their bond. Shoota and Musa's moms' names came up on the list to be placed in public housing. They were lucky to be moving in the same project buildings on 14th and W Street together. The two shared the same schools from elementary through high school. Shoota dropped out when his mom died of an overdose.

The reality of losing his mother was hard for Shoota. The pain he'd been through living with his mother wouldn't allow him the privilege to cry or mourn her death until Shoota's mom was lowered in the ground, a part of Shoota was lowered into that grave with her.

Musa's mom Cheryl was a recovering addict, living in the shelter with Shoota's mom Renee. They became very close. Cheryl tried to encourage Renee to get clean for Shoota's sake, but the power of addiction was too strong for Renee. That forced Shoota to spend a lot of time at Cheryl and Musa's apartment when they lived on W.

Street. Cheryl loved Shoota like he was her own son. Musa loved Shoota like he was his little brother. The two were inseparable.

After Renee passed, Cheryl wanted to adopt Shoota, but being as though she had a past of addiction and was a struggling mom, on public assistance D.C.P.S gated the adoption. That placed Shoota in a position to duck DCPS for two years until he turned eighteen. Shoota refuse to be housed anywhere other than with Cheryl and Musa.

During those times that Shoota was avoiding capture from the Department of Child protection service, Cheryl and Musa harbored, fed, and clothed Shoota.

Shoota and Musa's bond was tight, so Shoota couldn't understand why Musa hadn't told him how he came across the five kilos.

"Aye, Mu, you gonna lace a brother up on how you stumbled on five bricks?" Shoota asked, breaking the silence in the car.

Musa looked ahead, navigating the Chrysler through traffic. Shoota could see Musa's eyes turn into a dead man's stare that reflected pain, and just that quick it vanished. Musa hit the backwood again before passing it back to Shoota.

"Come on, Shoota. Do I gotta tell you everything that's going on with me? Shit at least a nigga ain't leaving you with an empty plate. You're gonna eat right along with me," Musa said, licking his lips.

The loud pack had his lips drier than a crackhead's feet.

"You don't have to tell me everything, just the important shit Musa. You may be two years older, but I'm way too hip to be slow, my nigga. I know you even bodied a nigga or two for them five joints or you stole a nigga's stash. I just wanted to be on point if a nigga comes lurkin' about this shit."

"No one is coming lurking. I can promise you that, slim..." Musa paused.

"Do you trust me, Shoota?" Musa asked.

"What type of question is that, Musa? You know I trust you with my life," Shoota stated slightly offended.

"Well, let sleeping dogs lie on this one and let's just get this money. How's the spot turning out?" Musa asked

"It's a little slow but shits moving," Shoota said, pulling a zip-loc bag out of his dip that contained big faced $5 bills.

He started removing more money from his socks and the bottom of his shoes.

Musa balled his face up like he'd just smelled the worst thing ever. "Nigga, put ya muthafuckin' shoes back on. Your feet smell like hot ass and boiled eggs.

"Nigga, what you smell is that grind to success. Since we cut them two bricks into nickels two weeks ago all I've been doing is fuckin' Cookie and grinding nonstop." Shoota smiled, stuffing the money back in his shoes before placing them back on his feet.

"I told myself I'm not showering until I sell the first key."

Musa respected Shoota's hustla ambition, but the boy's feet stink like old and new shit. Shoota was hungry and his grind was real. Musa, Shoota and Ace had made an agreement that they would bust two bricks down into nickel bags but make them big enough to sell as dimes if they wanted to. It was all in the plan to jump start the clientele, once they were finished with the first brick they would come together, bust down the money and work the other three bricks into cash. From there their goal was to find a connect to invest their money into more products through all the planning the trio did that night, somehow Money Mafia was birthed.

"Aye, fam, we about to pull up on Fat Corey," Musa informed.

As he bent the corner on 7th and Taylor Street. Shoota's head moved in a swirl motion trying to peep the scene. He stuffed the ziploc bag under his seat that contained the money.

Musa surveyed his surrounding until he spotted Fat Corey par-laying in front of one of the many abandoned houses that dotted Taylor Street. Musa put the .380 in his back pocket and removed the fourteen grams of hard from under the dashboard.

"I'm only gonna be a minute," Musa said, climbing out of his car.

"Yeah, homie make it quick. I don't even like the way shit is set up around here," Shoota complained. Musa ignored him.

Fat Corey watched Musa get out of his car and cross the street to where he stood with a few fiends. When Musa approached Fat

Corey, he noticed One-Punch amongst them. One-Punch was one of the crackheads that didn't look like the other fiends who roamed Washington D.C. He looked like the everyday hustler, but he wasn't. One-Punch was famous for knocking out niggas for a hit of coke. He didn't discriminate who he knocked out. All he cared about was the rock he was going to smoke once he knocked your ass out. Seeing One-Punch made Musa leery.

"What's up, Musa? I see ya brought Shoota with ya," Fat Corey stated nodding his head toward Shoota who was waiting in the car watching all movement like a gambler at a dice game.

"Fuck all that let's get to the business, my nigga," Musa replied watching the group's body language.

"Where them grams at, slim?" Fat Corey asked for some reason the octave in his voice had change.

"Money first," Musa instructed

"Damn, slim you done came up on a few grams. Now you don't trust a nigga. Boi they say when a broke nigga start making moves, he'll change in a blink of an eye," Fat Corey's statement was laced with a little malice.

"Come on, fat boi. I don't even trust God when it comes to my paper. So, just come with the dough so I can get in traffic."

Creases fell on Fat Corey's forehead from the words that came out of Musa's mouth. Fat Corey nodded at One-Punch who dug in the pocket of his Polo sweatpants and removed a small roll of money. He tossed it to Musa.

Musa caught the money in mid-air and started counting it soon as it hit his hands.

Before he could finish his count Fat Corey interrupted his count. "Aye, Musa, cough them grams up and stop playing with a nigga."

Musa didn't even pay the energy in Fat Corey's voice attention. He just dug in his pocket, removed the fourteen grams of hard and tossed it to the man that paid him the five hundred. This infuriated Fat Corey.

"Aye, Musa, you disrespecting me, homie?"

"Naw, I'm not disrespecting. I'm just serving the nigga who handed me the money," Musa stated nonchalantly while he began recounting the money.

Nightfall was falling on the District but that didn't stop Musa from seeing the digits on the bills he was counting or the change in the atmosphere around him. When he looked up from the short money he'd just counted, he had enough time to dip his head to the right to protect his jaw from the solid right One-Punch threw his way. The blow connected to the left side of Musa's head. The punch didn't knock him out, but it rocked Musa sending him falling backward.

Musa's body went into survival mode and while he was in transition of falling back, his hand came out of his back pocket with the .380. He rode the trigga as he fell back.

Boom! Boom! Boom! Boom!

The money Musa had in his hand flew in the air as bullets zipped past One-Punch and Fat Corey. The block scattered for cover right along with the two muthafuckas Musa was desperately trying to kill.

Boom! Boom! Boom!

Musa laid on the pavement with an empty gun, dazed.

"Musa, get up! You good?" Shoota asked as he helped his friend to his feet.

Musa's thoughts was a little cloudy but he managed to shake the cloudiness off, picked up the scattered money and the fourteen grams that One-Punch had dropped. Musa and Shoota jogged to the waiting Chrysler and pulled out.

Musa hit a few side streets before he emerged on the avenue heading back toward Ledroit Park.

"Damn, slim, my head is hurting like a muthafucka," Musa said, touching his forehead where One-Punch had hit him.

He could feel the large warm knot that sat on the side of his head. He looked in the mirror to examine the damage. That's when he saw twelve behind him.

"Fuck!" Musa yelled.

"What?" Shoota asked, alarmed.

He glanced in the side mirror and his heart dropped when he saw the police behind them. Musa floored the car and the police lit blue and red on its roof. Musa's Chrysler 300 was no match for the souped up engine, the police had under its hood.

No matter what Musa tried to do, he could not loose twelve, as came down Georgia Avenue to the intersection of Florida Avenue. D.C police cars boxed Musa and Shoota in. Musa slammed on brakes bringing the car to a screech halt.

The whole scene went into slow motion like a motion picture. Musa and Shoota watched the surrounding officers draw their weapons when they exited their police cruisers. They stood behind open car doors with their weapons pointed at Musa and Shoota. Musa's heart beat hard, his mind flashed to him serving a long prison bid for the attempted to murder, drugs and the .380 that he had in the car with him. Musa's mind was so dumbfounded over what he may be facing, he didn't hear the officer's instruction to exit the vehicle and lay face down on the ground. He didn't hear what Shoota was saying until Shoota hit his leg bringing him out his trance.

"Give me the tool, nigga!" Shoota demanded with his hand out. Shoota's eyes were on the police that had him boxed in.

"Huh! What?" Musa said not comprehending what Shoota was saying.

"Give me the damn tool. I'll take the gun charge for you, my nigga."

Musa's face balled into a knot of ugliness. "Fuck nawl, nigga. I got this shit," Musa stated sternly.

"Nigga, dem crackas gonna smoke ya boots if they bag you with dat burner and dem fourteen grams. I'll plea to the gun and you, plea to the drugs. We'll be back at it in no time," Shoota pleaded with eyes of tears.

Musa stared in the eyes of Shoota and his heart swelled. Shoota was like a little brother to him. He was the one that should have been making big brother sacrifices for Shoota, but it was the other way around. Shoota was demonstrating that he had real love for him, but Musa was hesitant.

"Shoota, I can't, bruh!"

"Nigga, if they take you away from me I have nothing, Musa. You all I got, bruh," Shoota said sincerely.

Musa felt like a pussy for even contemplating what he was. But he knew Shoota was right. If he got caught with drugs and guns it was a wrap. He would be facing a Fed bid. Musa took a deep breath and reluctantly passed Shoota the .380. When Shoota's hand touched the gun, Musa wouldn't let it go. He and Shoota locked eyes both held tears.

"Love you, my nigga," Musa mouthed

Shoota capped back, "That's what Money Mafia is based on, love. A minor sat back for a major come back." Shoota took the gun out of Musa's hand and exited the car.

***

When Shoota came back to the presence he found himself back in the parking lot of the Stadium Strip Club. He wiped the moisture from his face, grabbed his phone from between the seats and sent a text.

//: Let's play chess.

Immediately a smiling emoji came back with devil horns.

"Money Mafia is mine," Shoota mumbled exiting the Benz wagon to see what the Stadium night life had to offer besides Jassii.

Chapter 4

Musa stood in the middle of his spacious walk-in shower; his arms folded with his hands tucked under his armpits. The four-way high pressure shower head rained hot water on his body giving his tensed muscles great relief. Musa held his head down with his eyes closed. He'd gotten little sleep last night. He tossed and turned all night. The episode with Shoota and how he conducted himself wouldn't allow him a wink of sleep. That inner alarm that every real street nigga has in them was ringing loud and clear. No matter how much his mind and heart reminded him of the love he had for Shoota it wasn't enough to silence the alarm.

Musa deactivated the shower heads from the keypad located on the wall. The keypad had multiple options for you to partake in doing your shower depending on your needs and desires. Snatching the bottle of Dove Men + Care Body & Face wash. He placed a large amount on his washcloth and thoroughly scrubbed his body. The micro moisture and purifying grains the bodywash contained made his skin tingle. The smell the body wash held waffled up Musa's nose granting him that aromatherapy that he needed to loosen the tension in his body. After rinsing the suds off, Musa stepped out of the shower and dried himself with a towel designed by Gucci.

Musa walked over to the mirror over the sink and wiped the shower steam from it. A pair of red eyes stared back at him. He ran his hand over his two-week old fade and low beard. Musa wasn't considered handsome; he was what many chicks called fair looking. The way he carried himself was more alluring than his looks. The pair of gray eyes that he was gifted with was handed down from his father. The women found deep fascination in them. The fact that he was six-feet even and the color of Hershey syrup contributed to his cockiness which made the women love him so dearly.

Musa knew he had a lot of shit to do today but he made a mental note to swing by the barbershop, get his fade tightened and get a fresh line on his beard. Musa stroked a palm brush over his head, laying his waves down. He went onto handling his hygiene.

Musa chose to dress light today, he chose a pair of black 501 jeans, a white V-neck Versace shirt with the black Medusa head stamped on the front of it and a size 11 throwback black and white Bo Jacksons and a splash of Polo Blue on his skin. Lastly, he dropped the double M chain over his neck. He studied himself in the full-length mirror and felt like the fit was missing something. Walking to his dresser top he chose an all-platinum Movado watch that put everything into perspective.

Heading downstairs, Musa grabbed his phone off the charger and checked for any missed calls. He had a few from a few chicks he was smashing and a few pics of them in sexy bodysuits or thongs with captions encouraging him to pull up on them. Musa made another mental note to get with this chick that had been begging him to get with her. She sent him a picture of her and another chick kissing who was Megan The Stallion thick.

The picture came in with an attachment that read: *ALL WE NEED IS U.* Musa stored the pic in his picture gallery and deleted the rest.

Musa open a picture text from Shoota. He was at the strip club wilding the fuck out solo with a busload of strippers dancing around him and money floating in the air.

The text read: *//: Boss of bosses.*

Musa didn't know what bothered him the most. The words in Shoota's text or the fact that Jassii was standing in the background of the picture watching Shoota with a mug on her face. If the situation from last night would never have surfaced, Musa wouldn't even be experiencing the emotion he was feeling. He would have just taken the text as his boy being turned all the way up last night Money Mafia style. Musa's heart was heavy thinking about the whole ordeal.

Bzzzz! Bzzzz! Bzzzz!

Musa's other burner phone vibrated on the table. Only one person had this number, that person was the only individual that ever called the phone.

"Papaya, my friend," Musa stated answering the phone.

"How's things going with you, Musa, my friend?"

28

"Living a dream but praying that it don't become a nightmare," Musa retorted.

Papaya could hear the distress in Musa's voice and he became alarmed.

"What's going on, Musa? Talk to me," Papaya stated trying to draw out of Musa what was burdening his heart.

Musa and Papaya's relationship was deeper than business. It was out of love and respect. So, Musa wasted no time conveying the current events to Papaya. He and Papaya had become close like father and son would. Papaya always gave Musa the type of advice that was food of thought and helped him grow with life lessons. Papaya was a master in observance and listening. Since he wasn't able to see Musa. He applied his listening skills and only interrupted to ask a question here and there, so he could get a full understanding of what was going on.

When Musa finished telling Papaya everything, he wanted him to know about the situation with Shoota. There was a long pause over the phone.

"Hello," Musa said thinking he may have lost connection.

"I'm here, Musa," Papaya said in a hush tone. "A great man by the name of Sun Tzu once stated, *"Don't depend on the enemy not coming, depend on being ready for him."*

"But Papaya, I'm not talking about an enemy. I'm talking about a friend, a brother. I'm talking about a person who sacrificed a few years of his life in a cage for me," Musa corrected in defense of Shoota.

"Life's greatest dangers often come not from external enemies, Musa, but from our supposed colleagues, friends, and family who pretend to work for the common cause while scheming to sabotage us. Your friend has a cancer in him. I don't know if this the same cancer that made Sammy the bull betray John Gotti or the same sickness that made Alpo flip on Wayne Perry. But whatever it is, it must be removed, or it will harm you and those around you. Listen, my friend, I know these are some hard choices you have to make, but I've been on this phone longer than I'm supposed to. The C.O.

is making rounds, keep me informed. Your money was received, and the shipment will be there in two days."

The line went dead, Musa wasn't nearly ready to get off the phone with Papaya. He wanted to stay on the line so Papaya could help him workout his problem.

Musa was more confused about his situation than he was before Papaya called. Musa twisted him a Bob Marley size blunt and went and dropped a baby mouse in the fifty-five-gallon tank that was used to house Musa's giant Tarantula. As soon as the mice hit the bottom of the tank, the tarantula pounced on its prey and sunk his poisonous fangs in it. The mouse became instantly paralyzed as the huge Arachnid started the process of turning the rodent insides to mush and sucking them out like it was a milkshake. Musa watched in excitement, but it was the sad realization that he may have to deal Shoota the same fate.

**

"Oh, shit," Ace purred as she lost herself with her toes curling feeling Jassii's tongue all over her swollen clit.

Jassii smiled as Ace's juices coated her mouth and chin like an invisible goatee. Jassii's horizon was a sexy valley of pussy, stomach, and titties. Ace bit down on her bottom lip while Jassii feasted on her pussy like she was starving and had just been granted her last meal. Ace arched her back off the California King size bed. Her body trembled when the thunderous orgasm rocked through her like a tsunami causing her to clamp her thighs around Jassii's head.

When Jassii inserted her long tongue in Ace's back door, swirling around her sphincter, Ace climaxed back-to-back. At that moment, Ace learned the real definition of a rim job. Jassii felt her lover shake and go limp, she knew she had Ace riding the cloud of ecstasy, which gave her ultimate satisfaction. Jassii removed her tongue and kissed Ace on the bottom of her butt cheeks. The craving to be penetrated came over her. Jassii immediately became guilty knowing that only hours ago she'd allowed Shoota to beat her guts

30

like he'd just come home from prison. Shoota left her twat sore and swollen.

Jassii made her way to the bathroom for a noon shower which would allow Ace a moment to herself. Ace blew air out of her mouth and wiped the light coat of sweat from her forehead and nose.

Ace's thighs were still slightly quivering. She laid there for the next several minutes trying to regain her composure. Her mind was blown, she and Jassii were in a relationship for years now and Jassii had never blessed her with her tongue in the booty. She enjoyed the experience and definitely wanted to experience Jassii tongue in her dookie chute.

Ace couldn't help but wonder if Jassii was cheating on her and picked up the sex act from one of the nasty bitches that she worked with at the club. She quickly suppressed her thoughts, she refused to allow her thoughts to make her insecure. So, Ace climbed out of bed and worked a pair of white Victoria Secret boy shorts over her hips and pulled a pink wife beater over her head and breasts. Ace entered the kitchen of her three-bedroom $800,000 mansion. The house was located off Whelan Lane out Potomac Maryland. The kitchen was her favorite place in the house everything was black marble and stainless steel. The kitchen came with a stove and grill island that sat in the middle of the kitchen.

Ace had no plans of cooking today. It was way after twelve and she had shit to do. So, she removed four small microwavable breakfast bowls from the fridge and popped them into the microwave two at a time. She poured V-8 juice in two glasses, set them on the counter and waited for the Jimmy Dean breakfast bowls to heat up.

Jassii entered the kitchen wearing a body suit that snapped together between the legs. The body suit was white with pink Louis Vuitton lettering on it. The one piece was eaten up by Jassii's backside, but the front revealed her creases and her clit piercing could be seen through the Louie Vuitton fabric. Jassii already had her first cherry flavored backwood of the day burning in between her fingers.

"Ooohhh, that smells good!" Ace announced smelling the sweet scent of the hemp burning.

"This that tropical Kush here. My brother hit me off with it last night when he stopped through the club to drop the dancers a few pills off."

The mention of Jacob being at the club angered her knowing that Jassii didn't call and let her know that her brother was at the club. Jassii knew she was trying to contact Jacob about them two bricks she fronted Jacob.

"I know one of those breakfast cups is mine?" Jassii asked, catching a whiff of the eggs and sausages cooking in the microwave.

"We got two a piece!" Ace stated thinking about how she was going to address the situation about Jassii.

Beep! Beep! Beep!

The microwave sounded, Jassiii handed Ace the backwood and retrieved the breakfast bowls. She reloaded the microwave with the two awaiting breakfast bowls and set the timer on the microwave for three minutes.

Ace watched Jassii's back side until she took a squat on a stool at the counter and started mixing her eggs and sausage in the bowl. The stool Jassii sat on was eaten whole by her mammoth ass cheeks. Ace smiled, thinking nasty thoughts. She took a long pull of the backwood filling her lungs whole. She let smoke slowly seep from her nose and let the Kush kick in before she went in on Jassii.

"Jacob never cleared that debt he accumulated with me," Ace stated through a cloud of smoke.

Jassii hated when Ace talked like she had a legit business when she wasn't nothing but a drug dealer. Jassii rolled her eyes, getting annoyed. Ace watched Jassii and didn't miss the fact that Jassii rolled her eyes once she made her statement.

"Come on, Ace, you know he's gonna pay you. I guess he's trying to run the check up before he pays you."

"Jassii, he's had four months to run the checkup. Your bro on some fuck shit. And I'm telling now, ain't no nigga fucking me outta my paper. He even fucked the work up or he's preying on the fact that I'm your bitch and nothing will come to him for being on the bullshit."

"What you gonna do kill my brother like you did yours?" Jassii stated in bewilderment.

The statement brought extra creases to Ace's forehead. She never thought the one that she loved would ever use her deepest darkest secrets against her. If Ace's enchanting gray eyes could kill, Jassii would have been a dead bitch, but Ace cuffed her feelings on the matter.

"Jassii, you wrong for bringing that up, but let's not get off subject. Your brother owes me sixty bands. I want my money from his clown ass."

"Pssssttt, the money that the Mafia be making is peanuts compared to what my brother owes you from what y'all be rackin in," Jassii stated firmly stuffing a fork full of eggs and sausages in her mouth.

Ace knew right then she had violated by allowing herself to pillow talk with Jassii and even doing business with her woman's brother.

"You know what, bae, you're right that's small change to what Money Mafia is making," Ace said walking over and kissing Jassii on the lip. She gave her backside a light pat. Ace started to exit the kitchen.

"Where you going? You haven't eaten," Jassii inquired.

"I'm gonna finish this backwood in the tub while I'm soaking. Then I'm going to come back and eat me something," Ace said.

"Ace!" Jassii called out.

"Yeah."

"I'm sorry about bringing your brother into our shit."

"Me too!" Ace said walking out of the kitchen.

Once Ace made it to her bedroom, her she-devil horns poked from her head and went into savage mode. She located Jassii's phone in her Prada bag. She went through her contacts finding Jacob's name, she sent him a quick text.

//: Hey, bro, I just clipped two bricks from my bitch's stash. Meet me at Grandma's in an hour and come get this shit. ~Jassii~

Instantly, Jassii's phone buzzed in Ace's hand. It was Jacob's clown ass. Ace opened the text.

//: WTF! Not over the phone. Meet U N an hour! ~Jacob~

"Greedy bitch!" Ace mumbled deleting the message from Jassii's phone.

She grabbed her phone off the nightstand and sent Brim a text. Ace hopped into black leggings and slid her feet into pink and black Jordans. She grabbed a black hoodie, along with her Glock 17. She put the gun on her hip, and was ready to go.

"Hey, Jassii, some shit came up. I need to meet Musa about some shit. Do you want to push the Porsche today? I'll drive your car?"

Jassii didn't hesitate switching cars with Ace. She'd been dying to get behind the wheel of the 911 Porsche. Ace tongued Jassii after they swapped keys then jumped behind the wheel of Jassii's Lexus and murked out.

Money Mafia

Chapter 5

"Brim, baby, when ya gonna let me rock ya chain?" Cynthia asked standing on her back legs in a way only a true project chick could do.

Cynthia stood between Brim's legs as he leaned against his cocaine white Lexus truck. The truck looked villain-like resting on all black 28-inch rims. Cynthia held the diamond out double M charm in the palm of her hand. The charm filled the palm of her hand and she liked the weight it had to it. All the diamond karats made the lining of her panties gushy.

"Soon as you let a nigga fuck something!" Brim replied with a straight face.

He was used to being straight with bitches telling them what it was. Money was the fuel behind it. Being a member of Money Mafia had his confidence all the way up.

"Boi, you better stop playing because you can get the business like its 7-11, twenty-four hours any time of the day," Cynthia seductively replied biting down on a manicured fingernail that she placed between her two front teeth. Brim reached between Cynthia's thick thighs and massaged her love box through the pink leggings she wore.

Cynthia was one of them older broads in the hood that had a thing for young goons and hustlas getting money. The rumor was that Cynthia fucked like a porn star and the pussy and head was awesome. Brim wanted to see if the rumor was true or false.

"Where we gonna do this at?" Brim asked feeling the heat radiating from between Cynthia's legs.

"Brim, you's not ready. I'm telling you if I let your young ass hit, you gonna try and wife a bitch," Cynthia said, stepping closer in Brim's personal space.

She moved Brim and guided it inside her leggings and panties. She was extra wet, Brim moved two fingers in and out of her creases feeling the silkiness of her lady lips between his fingers.

The hustlers that occupied the front of Ledroit Park buildings had a hard time paying attention to their surroundings and the drug traffic because of the performance Brim and Cynthia was putting on.

Brim pulled his fingers out of Cynthia's honey pot; a sticky dew was coating his fingers. He placed them under his nose and made eye contact with Cynthia.

"Nigga, go ahead my poo-nanny is Gucci," Cynthia stated guaranteeing that her love box was up to par.

Brim took a whiff; Cynthia's scent was on point. Her garden had a light musk scent, not that funky musk scent, but the kind that activated a man's hormones and made him want to fuck something.

Brim removed the coochie stain fingers from under his nose and place them in Cynthia's mouth, she didn't hesitate to suck them clean.

"Now what?" Cynthia said popping Brim fingers out of her mouth.

Brim's manhood grew harder than Pinocchio's nose after he'd told a vicious lie.

"Shit we don't have to make this shit difficult we can do the deed in your crib," Brim said in a mannish tone.

Cynthia had so many ways she was gonna put the pussy on Brim. She knew when she was finished with him, Brim would be treating her to them greenbacks he keeps in his pocket. Cynthia grabbed the young hustla by the hand and led him up the walkway toward her building she strutted along the way giving a show of her butt cheeks and received a round of applause with every step she took.

Bzzz! Bzzzz! Bzzzz!

Brim's vibrating phone in his back pocket made him shake his hand free from Cynthia's grasp to see who was calling him. He was willing to spend a few dollars on Cynthia, but he wasn't willing to miss any money fucking with her. He saw that it was Ace texting him. He thought about ignoring her text, but he decided against it. He opened the text.

//: Got Jas's bro N-A- Trick bag. MEET ME IN N.E. behind 21ˢᵗ Street on M Street A.S.A.P. I'M ENROUTE. ~Ace~

"Aye, Cyn, a nigga got to fuck with you later," Brim said walking away from Cynthia like she was yesterday's news.

Brim got into his truck and pulled out. Cynthia stomped her feet on the concrete and pouted like a child would do as she watched Brim's truck bend the corner.

"You should have been made a nigga aware that this bamma ass nigga was on some bullshit, Ace," Brim said from the back seat of Jassii's Lex.

The car had black interior and 35% tints on the car windows making the car insides dark and hard to see into.

"I know, Brim, but I was thinking that Jassii being my girl and she's the one that co-signed for him to get the front. He wouldn't play these fuck games. I guess I was wrong?"

"Do you think Jassii knew her brother was gonna pull this stunt?" Brim balled and unballed his fists.

Ace had suspicions about Jassii and the role she played in all of this. Her suspicion was aroused when Jassii was so nonchalant about Jacob not returning her calls when she was trying to collect her money. But Ace wouldn't straight up and admit this to Brim.

"I don't think so, Brim. I don't even want to think along those lines. If it wasn't for Jassii, I would have never fronted him the work let alone sold it to him."

Brim slightly shook his head disagreeing with Ace's statement. He felt Ace had let Jassii and their relationship cloud her better judgement on fronting Jassii's brother two bricks. Making moves like this shows that Ace was lacking in leadership. Shit like that was an insult to him. He understood why Shoota acted the way he did last night.

"Speak, what's on your mind, Brim? I see you back there shaking ya head," Ace stated watching Brim through the rearview mirror.

"Hold that shit down. I think that's our boi, right there," Brim said, nodding his head toward the red 2021 Range Rover sport pulling up on the other side of the street. "Damn, that nigga's riding good. You sure all you fronted him was two bricks?" Brim said, sliding down on the back seat.

Ace didn't even reply to Brim's slick ass comment. She just buried her face into the Christian Dior bag that she found on the passenger side floor in Jassii car. Ace could tell the bag was new because of the fresh leather smell and the price tag still attached to the bag. She never saw the blue and white CD bag before. She was the one who brought all Jassii's designer bags. For some reason Ace felt that the bag and Jassii putting her tongue in her butt was connected. She had to push them thoughts in the back of her mind as she watched Jacob out the peripheral climb out his Range.

Ace and Brim was parked directly in front of Jacob and Jassii's grandma's building. Jassii had brought Ace over to visit her a few times. The street Jacob's grandma lived on was low traffic.

Jacob walked over to the passenger side of his sister's Lexus. He couldn't see directly in the car due to the tint on the car, but he could make out the silhouette of someone sitting in the driver seat who he assumed was Jassii being as though it was her car and knowing Jassii let no one drive her Lexus. He was sadly mistaken once he opened the passenger's door. He was halfway inside the car when he realized it wasn't Jassii behind the wheel and someone had a gun pointed at his head from the back seat.

***

Musa stepped out of Pimptown Barbershop on 2nd and Kennedy Street NW. He walked to the double-parked black Maserati. Musa liked his cars like he liked his women, *black*. He had a thing for black cars with crimson red on the inside. The double M chain around his neck did the money dance under the sunrays. Musa hopped behind the wheel of the Maserati and burned out into traffic like the Maserati didn't cost more than a house.

Money Mafia's boss checked his fresh cut in the rearview, satisfied at how his cut looked he placed his eyes back on the road. It was funny how a fresh haircut could make a man's spirits rise. Everything going on with Shoota had him in a slump. The wedge that started growing between them over the last few months had been taking a toll on him. All the bullshit seemed to occur when Ace came into play. He was headed to Shoota's crib to have a talk with him about the tension that had been harvesting between them.

Money Mafia was getting money like it was The Reagan era. Papaya had them eating harder than BMF and he refused to let some bullshit come between them and fuck up their money flow. If Shoota knew why he made Ace his right hand and not him maybe he would have adjusted his mindset and embrace them facts cold heartily.

Just because Musa was trying to unscramble things in his head didn't mean he was slipping and didn't notice White Impala on his trail after he pulled away from the barbershop. He inconspicuously watched the Impala that was three cars back. Musa cruised down to 1st and Kennedy. He got caught at the light in front of Wings & Things. He eased the .45 Sig Sauer off his hip and made sure he had one in the chambers.

The Impala was too far back to determine who was behind the wheel, but Musa could definitely tell whoever it was wasn't the law. The light turned green and Musa pushed the Maserati through the light making his way to Georgia Avenue. There were too many cameras on the Avenue to just start popping the Sig he had on his lap.

Musa was getting vexed that a nigga had the audacity to try him in his city. Musa hit Brim on the jack, but his phone went to voicemail. He then tried Ace and got the same result.

"Fuck!" Musa said letting his foot off the accelerator and let the Maserati coast at a moderate speed.

He wanted the driver of the Impala to get close enough to him so he could get a better look at whoever was following him, but the driver kept their distance.

Musa hit Shoota's line, Shoota's phone rung four times before he answered, "What, Mu, I'm busy!" Shoota stated dryly.

Musa ignored Shoota's tone. "Nigga, I got someone following me, Shoota!" Musa stated out loud so Shoota could hear him. He had the phone on speaker.

"What! Where you at, slim?" Shoota had raw concern in his voice.

"I'm on Georgia Ave."

"I'm coming to you, Mu, stay on the line with me I'm around Ledroit Park."

"Nawl stay put and set the trap in the alley behind the building. I'm headed that way," Musa said, placing his foot back on the accelerator.

Ten minutes later, Musa bent the corner on 1st Street. The white Impala was directly behind him now. Once Musa got on the side street there wasn't any more cars between them and Musa still couldn't get a good look at who was following him. The driver of Impala had their sunvisor down and they were hiding their face behind it.

Musa didn't give a fuck now who was following him. If a muthafucka had followed him all the way to the park. Made it clear they were there to bring harm to him. Musa turned the Maserati into the alley behind the Ledroit Park building that the Impala pulled in behind him. Musa still had Shoota on the line.

"You see me, Shoota?" Musa said letting the car drift slowly through the alley.

"Yeah, I see ya keep coming down the alley and stop by the black gate."

Musa followed Shoota's instructions and stopped at the black gate. The Impala stop a few feet behind Musa. Two gunmen stepped out of the cut on opposite sides of the Impala they lifted the AR-15 and took aim.

"Hold!" A shout rung out and the two gunmen faded back into the cut.

Musa saw the police car turned into the alley. Shoota was watching from the roof of the building. He was the one who called off the shooters once he saw twelve turned in the alley.

Musa tapped the accelerator of the Maserati and brought the car to the end of the alley. His heart rate was up. Thinking how close he was to being a scene of a murder while the police was there. He made a right once he exited the alley. The Impala made a left.

Musa doubled around the block twice before he parked. He wanted to get with Shoota so they could brainstorm about what had just happened. Musa wasn't taking kindly to feeling like he was prey in his own city.

Jibril Williams

Chapter 6

Papaya got off the phone with Musa hours ago but he was still seated on his bunk. His mind and heart was burdened with the dilemma Musa was in. Even though Papaya never met Shoota personally, he had heard many things about Shoota through Musa. Many of them things was good and told Papaya that Musa had a solid soldier on his team, but what Musa conveyed to him about Shoota today reminded him of his past situation. Papaya was aware of those like Shoota. The one that claimed to love you but had hidden agendas. Their hidden agendas were fueled by jealousy and greed.

Papaya was a true testament to this; he was placed in prison for four terms of life without parole because his brother Castro professed that he was a brother's keeper. Papaya's brother Castro was two tongued. He confessed his oath of silence and loyalty but behind Papaya's back rallied Papaya's people against him. In the end, Castro couldn't run the family business in the manner that Papaya could. Castro was sloppy and with sloppiness came two things, mistakes and the FEDs.

When the FEDs came lurking with secret indictments. Castro turned state evidence becoming a rat. Castro gave the FEDs enough info to condemn Papaya to life in prison. Papaya leaned his back against the wall. He laced his fingers together and twirled his thumbs around one another. He was thinking what type of assistance would be necessary to make sure Musa came out on top of this situation.

A person like Shoota could only cause two types of problems, death or a lifetime of incarceration and both would cause Papaya to lose millions of dollars. It took Papaya years after Castro's betrayal to resurrect his cartel. Unknowingly to Musa he was a major player in Papaya's cartel and Musa didn't even know it. Papaya liked it like that. In another year Papaya had plans for Musa to be the number one supplier on the East coast, once he strategically eliminated his competition. Papaya and Musa became very close to doing those three years Musa spent in Wacken Hunt CAA private prison in NC.

Papaya wasn't a big fan of African Americans but he had the honor to see something in Musa so he invested his time in Musa, and eventually brought Musa into the folds of his organization. There was too much at stake to sit on the side lines and just watch the unthinkable unfold with Musa. Papaya fished his iPhone 7 from under his pillow and place a call.

Chapter 7

Musa parked in front of the Ledroit Park buildings. He played his mirrors, watching for any sight of the white Impala. Musa was vigilant with the .45 gripped in his hand while it rested on his lap. He really wished the police wouldn't have shown up when they did. If not, he would have had the answers of who was following him and why. He sent Ace a quick text telling her he was around L.P. and she needed to get with him asap. Ace responded back quickly saying that she and Brim would be pulling up in about two minutes.

Musa watched the scene in his mirrors. The Impala was nowhere in sight, but that didn't stop Musa from having an uneasy feeling in the pit of his stomach. Musa employed street team control and served the fiend that came through Ledroit Park project buildings to cop their choice of drugs. The hustler around Ledroit Park sold everything from coke to Heroin. Nothing looked out of place but the hairs on the back of his neck wouldn't lay down. He saw Brim's Lexus truck bend the corner and park behind him, then a purple Lexus parked right behind Brim's truck.

Musa knew the Lexus belonged to Jassii because she was the only one in the city that had a purple Lexus. Brim got out of his truck and Musa got out of his Maserati with the sig in his hand. Musa saw Ace climb out of Jassii's Lexus.

"What's going on, slim?" Brim asked, walking up to Musa. He had a concerned look in his eyes.

"I'll let you know when we get inside," Musa replied walking toward one of the buildings.

Shoota called from the roof of the building to let him know that's where he was. The hustlers were so into getting money and immune to seeing guns that no one paid much thought to why their boss had his burner out by his side. They just took his sight as their boss just being cautious.

When Musa, Brim and Ace made their way to the building rooftop. The trio was taken aback by the two unfamiliar faces and Musa didn't hesitate finding out who they were.

"Who the fuck is these niggas, Shoota? Why are they here?" Musa inquired.

Immediately creases fell upon Shoota's forehead. Musa's tone and line of questioning had him feeling some type of way. "These my B-more niggas that I was telling you about. This is Money and Bumps."

Rage jumped in Musa's eyes. Ace could tell by the look and shade in Musa's eyes that Shoota's response wasn't something Musa wanted to hear. Ace knew nothing good would come from this.

Musa had been telling Shoota for months that he didn't want to meet none of his people from Baltimore. To have those same people standing in the heart of his hood was an insult to Musa and had him wanting to slap fire outta Shoota's face.

"You showing these niggas way too much. Get them niggas the fuck from around here," Musa ordered

"Hold up, slim, these the same niggas that was about to air that white Impala out for you without even knowing who the fuck you were. Show some fucking gratitude," Shoota words sent Musa into blind rage.

Without thinking Musa lifted the .45 sig and squeezed off two shots.

Boom! Boom!

A single shot hit Money and Bump's head, both bodies dropped simultaneously, blood from bumps head splattered Shootas' shit. He was standing the closest to Shoota.

"What the fuck, Musa? Man, you tripping bad, Mu!" Shoota said with murder in his eyes and the heart of a killer.

Brim watched from the side lines. This was something he couldn't intervene in. The roof door busted open and Ledroit Park shooters came through the door clutching hella artillery. Ace quickly waved them away and sent a text to their clean-up crew to come and remove the bodies.

"You said show some gratitude. Thank you, but no thank you!" Musa said to Shoota's dead friends who laid on Ledroit Park rooftop with parts of their heads missing.

"Musa, I don't know what type of fuck shit you on but—"

"Fuck shit! Nigga, who the fuck brings outsiders to their home front. Who introduces niggas to the plug? What type of nigga puts outsiders in position to body a potential threat without testing their loyalty? You the one on the bitch shit. Either you stupid or you have a hidden agenda. Which one is it?" Musa said getting in Shoota's face while still holding the .45 sig.

"I'm far from dumb, Musa. So, what you tryna say, I got snake in me? I'm on some cutthroat shit?" Shoota asked through clenched teeth.

Musa could smell the scent of Henny on his breath. Musa delayed his reply, giving Shoota the impression that he had to think about his question when his answer should have been automatic. So, Shoota didn't give Musa a chance to respond.

He hit Musa with another question. "Was a nigga cutthroat when I took that gun charge for you? Or was it the four years I spent in them cracka's prison behind you that made me cutthroat? Did I have snake in me when I stayed solid on your name when twelve came questioning about you shooting One-Punch, nigga? Speak on it! Or are you gonna shoot me in the head, too?"

So many emotions ran through Musa's mind at that very moment. The tension on the roof was smothering, it was hard to breathe. Shoota's words had Musa second guessing himself and actions.

Musa knew Shoota was down with him like four flat tires on a hooptie. Shoota had always demonstrated his love and loyalty toward him, but why was his alarm bells ringing nonstop when Shoota came into play.

"Shoota, you've been moving reckless as fuck lately, slim. You been hostile toward your own team. You been giving the impression at times that you can run Money Mafia better than what I'm doing."

"The problem is, Musa, you don't see the boss in me. All my life I've been under you. I went to jail for you. I work for you. I murdered for you. I sacrificed for you. It's always about you, Musa. When is it ever gonna be about me, slim? I wanted to branch out to

Baltimore, be my own boss, establish my own shit but you're holding me back!" Shoota yelled.

"I'm not holding you back!" Musa yelled at Shoota with the same intensity.

"If you not what the fuck is the problem, Mu?" Shoota stated pointing at the two dead Baltimore niggas.

Brim could relate to Shoota's struggle to be his own boss. He wasn't feeling living in another nigga's shadow for a lifetime. He wasn't gonna put his input in the mix. He had his own plans.

Musa looked over Shoota's shoulder at the two slain bodies. "You call that hindering you from being your own boss? I think I saved you from a lifetime of hardship. Fuck them niggas. B-more niggas can't be trusted," Musa stated muggin' Shoota.

He wasn't felling the idea that Shoota wanted to leave Money Mafia. How Musa saw it was that Shoota was eating good with the Mafia why branch off to do something else when shit with Money Mafia wasn't broke. Shoota's statement made him seem jealous of Musa's status as boss.

Papaya's statement invaded his thoughts, *"Life's greatest dangers often come not from external enemies, but from our supposed colleagues, friends and family who pretend to work for the common cause."*

A burning sensation occurred in the pit of Musa's stomach as he shook his head, mentally reviewing Papaya's haunting words.

"Fuck 'em, huh, Musa?" Shoota asked as he walked off bumping Musa's shoulder.

Musa stood there with a mug on his face. He looked over at Ace, she held nothing but empathy in her eyes. Brim held a darkness in his eyes. At that time the clean-up crew arrived to retrieve the bodies. The sky had just turned dark so there wouldn't be a task of moving the bodies. The clean-up crew quickly place the bodies in individual body bags. There was a dumpster sitting next to the building. The clean-up crew dropped both bodies in the dumpster next to the building like they were everyday trash. They then went down and retrieved the bodies from the dumpster, then placed them in the back of black cleaner's van and drove them away.

Money Mafia

Musa was stress to the core all he wanted to do was smoke a phat backwood and sort his problem out mentally. He exited the roof with and Brim behind him.

Jibril Williams

Chapter 8

Jassii zig zagged the Porsche through traffic like it was a high-powered remote-control car. She loved the power of the car and how sexy the car made her feel. Jassii sat behind the wheel with all the windows rolled down, her beautiful eyes hid behind a pair of pink Dior frames. *WAP* by *Cardi B* and *Megan Thee Stallion* thumped through the Porsche's speakers. Jassii wanted the whole city to see what a boss bitch looked like driving something sexy and foreign. She was really feeling herself. Jassii sang and snapped her fingers to the music. It was the perks like this that she obtained by fucking with Ace. She loved every bit of it, but the betrayal of creeping on Ace made her feel like shit. She couldn't shake her cravings for Shoota or the good wood he was serving her.

Ace had Jassii living like a queen. Ace spent stacks on her that no nigga would ever spend on her. Ace took her to places that she could only dream of going. Some of those places Jassii couldn't pronounce and she had to Googled just to find out its location. Jassii couldn't name one chick that came out of Washington D.C. Southeast that was bossing it up like she was. The only person she could think of was Blac China. Now that bitch did it on a whole different level. She tricked Kim Kardashian's brother Rob Kardashian to pump a baby in her.

Jassii wasn't a lightweight. She was making a big bag shaking her ass across the country and out of the country, but she love how Ace catered to her and all the extra perks that came with being Ace's lover. She knew if Ace ever found out about Shoota and her, Ace would stop all those perks or even worse cease her love. Jassii felt like no dick was good enough to lose Ace's love, so she had to find a way to break free from Shoota's magic stick.

It was already bad enough she had convinced Ace to front her brother Jacob some work. She then went behind Ace's back and made a deal with her brother. Jassii told her brother to pay her thirty bands for the two bricks that Ace fronted him and she would deal with Ace about the situation of him owing her. Jassii deposited the money in her account and kept it moving.

The crazy thing about the situation was Jassii didn't have to do what she did, but the cruddy Southeast bitch was in her and she couldn't resist the opportunity of the come up. Jassii had been blowing up Jacob's phone for the last twenty minutes trying to locate him. She bet this nigga was at the crib sleep from running the streets last night. She was trying to get him to meet her so he could grab his cut of the money from the pills he had dropped off to her last night at the club. Jassii also needed to reup on pills. So, she didn't mind going to Jacob's crib to get them. Driving the Porsche made it an adventure.

She pulled up to Jacob's crib on Parkwood Northwest. She was going to keep going because she didn't see his Range Rover parked in front of his house. What made her stop was that Jacob's front door was sitting ajar. Jassii wanted to see what the fuck was going on. She slowly walked up to the house with much suspicion.

Jassii looked around to see if anyone was watching her. The street was fairly quiet. A few of Jacob's neighbors sat on their porch enjoying the night weather. Jassii wondered if her brother's house got raided or something because Jacob was extra careful about leaving his house unsecured. She rushed into the house only to find that her brother's house was ransacked. Jassii's heart rate elevated, and an uneasy feeling entered her stomach.

"Jacob!" she called out.

She thought she heard something coming from the back of the house where the bedrooms were located.

"Jacob, is that you?" Jassii called out tiptoeing down the hall.

She heard the noise again, the noise sounded like a moan.

Jassii used her phone in her hand to call 9-1-1. Jacob's bedroom was on the right. The phone started ringing but the signal was lost as soon as the dispatcher came on the line. Again, a moan could be heard, and it came from Jacob's room.

Jassii peeked her head in Jacob's room, just like the living room shit was tossed everywhere. From where she stood, she could see directly into Jacobs' walk-in closet. She could see Jacob's safe wide open and empty. Jassii walk in the room looking for any signs of her brother. Her phone rung in her hand. It was the dispatcher calling her back

"Hello!" Jassii answered

"Hello, ma'am, did you call 9-1-1?" The dispatcher asked in a calm and concern voice.

"Yes, I'm at my brother's house at 1411 Parkwood Street Northwest and it looks like someone has broken in—"

"Hummm!" The sound came from behind Jassii who stopped talking to the dispatcher mid-sentence.

Jassii turned around. You could hear the dispatcher's voice coming through the phone asking Jassii what was going on.

Jassii saw nothing when she turned around but when she walked around the other side of Jacob's king size bed. That's when she let out a wailing scream.

"Noooooo! Noooooo!" She discovered a naked and beaten Jacob lying on the floor clinging to his life.

***

"Musa, what the fuck happen today?" Ace asked handing Musa a shot glass and a bottle of Patron.

After the incident took place on the Ledroit Park roof. Musa and Ace decided to head back to her house to talk about what transpired. Ace sat down on the couch next to Musa barefooted with her legs tucked under her.

Musa didn't respond immediately he set the glass down on the corner table next to the couch and opted to drink straight from the bottle of Patron. Ace watched as Musa's Adam Apple bobbed up and down and he consumed the clear liquor. For a quick second Ace was confounded by how impressive Musa looked. Her nipples quickly budded underneath the fabric of her pink wife beater.

"So much shit happened today, Ace," Musa finally said after he removed the Patron bottle from his lips.

Musa used his tongue to wipe away the extra liquor from his lips. The gesture made Ace's heart double a few beats. She distracted herself by taking a sip of Patron from her glass.

"Some muthafuckas got on my line today when I was leaving Pimptown Barbershop."

"What?" Ace asked in shock with creases forming in the skin of her forehead. Concern rested in her eyes.

"Yeah, some bitch ass nigga pushing a white Impala. I couldn't get a good look at whoever it was they were riding with their visor down and the car tints dark." Musa took another long swig from the Patron bottle.

Ace was furious that someone was trying Money Mafia on some hoe shit. *They must have a death wish,* she thought.

"I tried to call you and Brim to let y'all know what was shaking with me, but I couldn't get y'all on the line."

Ace remembered Musa calling her phone, but she was in the middle of fucking Jacob over and getting her sixty bands back that was owed to her.

"I hit Shoota's sucka ass up. We made a plan for me to come through the hood so we could ambush whoever was trailing me but the plot was thawed when a police car came through and fucked the move." Musa ran his hand over his freshly cut fade and took another sip of Patron. Musa could feel the effects of the liquor.

Ace shook her head in disbelief. She was wrecking her brain on who she knew that drove a white Impala, but she kept coming up blank. Ace and Musa were silent for a moment, lost in their own thoughts.

"I swear I don't want to body my nigga, Ace," Musa's words broke their silence.

Ace looked at Musa out of her peripheral, she couldn't make eye contact with him after hearing the statement.

"He's gonna come for my spot, Ace. You heard that nigga talking tonight. That nigga had straight envy in his eyes. Shoota's a snake, Ace," Musa slurred. You could tell the thought alone of Shoota betraying him angered him by the way his chest rose and fell at a rapid pace.

From Ace's own experience, she knew killing a friend or family member was a delicate situation, so she had to choose her words wisely. "Mu, you letting that Patron do the thinking and talking for you. Your love for Shoota is real so stop talking about putting him in a grave. You two are like brothers. The history between you two runs deeper than slave blood," Ace informed him.

"That nigga ain't acting like fam. He acting like a snake in the grass just waiting his opportunity to strike." Spit sprinkled from Musa's mouth as he talked with force in his words. "Money and power have a way of changing niggas morals and principles. Shoota's morals and principles changed. He's not about Money Mafia, he's about self." Musa took the bottle of Patron to the head again.

Ace could not sit there and allow Musa to plant his own seed of doubt in his mind about Shoota. That would only lead him down a road to kill Shoota.

"Musa, I'm not seeing Shoota as a threat. I see him as an asset. He's a man that has his own ambitions who wants to be his own boss. Come on, Musa, who doesn't want to control their own destiny?" Ace asked removing the bottle of Patron from his hand. She refilled her glass and gave the bottle back to him.

"Naw fuck that! It's Money Mafia all day every day or nothing!" Musa blurted out.

"See that's where you're wrong. Never hinder a man from his growth. And right now, you're hindering Shoota and he's getting frustrated. You've been denying Shoota assistance on the Baltimore move since he been speaking on it. Shoota just wants something for himself, why not let him branch out to Baltimore. He would run his own operation out there under the condition that he keeps Money Mafia's name, and you become his direct supplier. Think about it like this, the Mafia would be making more money by plugging into Baltimore. Shoota would have his own branch of Money Mafia and you won't have the blood of a friend on your hands or conscious." Ace stopped talking to see if what she was saying was making any sense to Musa.

Musa sat there with a long mug on his face contemplating everything Ace had said. Then the brightest smile ever appeared on his face. Seeing Musa's smile Ace figured Musa was in agreement.

"See that's why you are second in command. You give a nigga a different perspective about shit. I could see shit working out in everyone's favor with this move." Musa stood up from the couch.

Ace's phone had been buzzing nonstop for the last hour. She saw that it was Jassii calling again. Jassii must have found out that her brother had been beaten and robbed. She didn't want to deal with that right now. When Musa was concerned nobody came before him. Musa was her God, her unclaimed lover. Ace placed the phone face down on the coffee table that was in front of the couch and stood to her feet.

Musa stood about a foot away from her. Their eyes met and locked. It was bizarre how their gray eyes were similar. Musa's eyes turned a shade grayer. He closed the gap between them invading Ace's personal space. Her C-cups pressed against the bottom of Musa abs.

"What's this? What happened?" Musa asked running his fingers over the dark brown mark that laid across Ace's jaw line from the distant that Musa was standing the spot looked like a bruise, but now Musa was close up on it, he could tell it was blood.

When Musa's finger touched Ace's face Niagara Falls formulated between her legs if Jassii went down on her at this very moment she would need goggles.

"Whose blood is this?" Musa asked in a slur.

"It's probably Jacob's blood. Brim and I paid Jacob a visit today to collect that sixty bands he owed, that's why me and Brim didn't answer the phone when you called us."

The whole time Ace was talking Musa held her face in his hand. Musa stuck his thumb in her mouth and coated it with his saliva. He removed it and used it to wipe the dry blood from Ace's face. Normally Ace would never allow a man's spit to touch her face, but this was her God, her king and when it came to Musa he had no restrictions.

Ace could have sworn that she felt a trail of wetness running down her legs. How could this be when Ace was a lesbian. It was like time was on pause when Musa leaned forward and placed his lips on hers. Ace hungrily accepted Musa's tongue in her mouth.

Even though this kiss was short it wasn't short enough for Jassii to walk in and catch them in the act.

Jibril Williams

Chapter 9

"Bitch you in here cupcaking with this nigga while I've been blowing your phone up when I needed you the most." Jassii's sudden presence made Musa and Ace jump a part.

Jassii rushed Ace, catching her with a blinding slap to the face. One of Jassii's fingers hit Ace in the eye during the process bringing tears to her eyes. Ace wasn't going to let watery eyes cause her to lose a head up fade. Ace threw two punches blindly connecting one of those to Jassii's forehead. Musa backed up against the wall giving the women some space to thump.

Jassii stumbled back from Ace's blow, then rushed her and kicked her in the stomach folding Jassii over. Jassii hands and knees stopped her from falling on her face.

"Get the fuck up!" Ace yelled standing over top of Jassii.

Ace and Jassii had been lovers for over two years and the couple had plenty of arguments, but they never came to blows.

Ace's real anger came not from Jassii catching Musa and her kissing but the fact that she learned from Jacob the fuck shit Jassii was on by pocketing the thirty bands he had given her. But Ace would never mention that to Musa or in front of Musa.

Jassii struggled to her feet but the kick to her stomach had taken the fight out of her.

"Ace, I just want to get my shit and leave. My brother needs me right now. I don't have time for this shit right now. If you want to be with Musa, go right ahead," Jassii said standing to her feet and putting a protecting forearm over stomach.

Ace still held fight in her eyes, but she allowed Jassii pass her. She followed Jassii to the bedroom. She watched Jassii pack her things from the doorway. Ace didn't want Jassii to go, with each item she threw in the bag her heart shattered into pieces. Jassii stuffed as much stuff as she could in her Gucci luggage. Tears weld in Ace's eyes but she refused to let Jassii see her cry. She was mad at her for the shit she pulled with her brother. Jacob confessed everything when Brim and Ace was beating his ass. But with Jassii witnessing her and Musa kissing the time wasn't right to reveal those facts.

Jassii opened her safe and emptied its contents which was nothing but stacks of money and a few pieces of drip that Ace had purchased for her. Ace contemplated getting the thirty bands now from Jassii but she changed her mind.

"When we both calm down, I would like to have a talk with you. But whatever it's worth to you, what you saw with me and Musa is not what you think," Ace stated calmly.

Jassii didn't reply, she just kept packing her belongings. When she finished, she pushed pass Ace standing in the doorway of the bedroom. Daisy by Marc Jacob attacked Ace's nostrils as she past making Ace want to throw her arms around Jassii and beg for forgiveness but she held firm to her position. Ace followed Jassii to the front door. Musa was gone. Jassii stopped at the door and turned around to give Ace that, *I hate you* stare before she walked out.

Ace's eyes hurt and emotionally she felt like shit. Despite what happened with Jassii. Ace couldn't stop from loving her. Jassiii had been there at some critical points of her life. Like when Ace's mom passed away from ovarian cancer. Jassii was there through it all and for that Ace would always love Jassii. She wasn't ready to give up on Jassii and her relationship. Ace sat down on the couch and wondered if Jassii felt the same way about her. She wondered could things be repaired between the two. Just going over all these emotions made Ace ball up on the couch and cry her eyes out.

Chapter 10

Every time Brim pounded deep into Cynthia it caused his double M chain around her neck to slap against the naked skin of her Double D breasts. Brim had Cynthia on all fours on the edge of her queen size bed.

He had her jumbo size butt cheeks spread thin adding extra stretch marks to the ones that already decorated her butt. He watched in endearment at how his pipe was being devoured by Cynthia's twat with every thrust. Repeatedly he pushed and pulled out of Cynthia womb causing his wood to be even wetter than it was before he pushed in her. He could feel coochie juices coating his nut sack and trickle down his inner thighs.

"Fuck meeee, Brim! Please go deeper. I neeeeed it deeper!" Cynthia moaned out putting on her Oscar winning performance.

She had her back arched, throwing her ass back into Brim's pelvis matching every thrust. A light coat of sweat appeared on Brim's forehead and his legs began to shake. He pounded Cynthia harder. He was hoping he would bust soon because if he kept hammering into Cynthia the way he was, he was sure the magnum condom would break.

All the rumors about Cynthia getting it in like a porn star was dead on point. After the situation with Musa and Shoota, Brim didn't want to sit around and discuss the events. In his book what was done was done, no need sitting around talking about it. So, Brim told Musa and Ace that he had some moves to make and he would check in with them tomorrow. Brim thought he was going to bust a nut or two, but his encounter with Cynthia turned into an all-night affair, which bled over until the morning.

Cynthia did all kinds of tricks on the dick. She sucked while she stood in a handstand. She gave Brim every hole. No matter what position Brim pinned her in she begged for more pipe. Cynthia's head and tongue game was fiya, but her pussy was something furious. She had mad muscle control.

"Oh, baaaaby give it to me. Where that nut at? Come on, baby, give it to me." Cynthia cooed with the Money Mafia diamond chain still swinging and slapping against her breasts.

Brim stroked harder, he'd fucked so much last night he didn't think he could cum anymore. Cynthia's goodies was so good he just had to hit one more time before he left. Now he started thinking that was a bad mistake.

Brim wanted to tap out, but he refused to go down in the books as letting a project thot tap him out. So, he concentrated harder.

"Brim, I want you to cum in my mouth," Cynthia said over her shoulder at Brim.

She reached back between her legs and massaged Brim's-soaked nuts. That put Brim there. His wood stiffened; he could feel his thug passion rushing to the tip of the condom. In one swift motion Brim pulled out of Cynthia, snatching the condom off. Cynthia spun around on the bed with the quickness.

As soon as Brim's dick hit her warm wet mouth he sprayed her tongue with his man juices, the last he had in his body. Brim's eye rolled in the back of his head as the last centimeter of sperm oozed from his wood. Brim pulled out of Cynthia's mouth, staggered next to her on the bed and fell back. Brim fought hard to catch his breath.

Cynthia being ghetto professional, she wanted to provide good service and keep the person coming back. She went to the bathroom and came back with a toothbrush in her mouth and a damp washcloth. She wiped the sweat from Brim's forehead and chest then she cleaned the coochie residue away from his now deflated member. Any other time if a woman would have done this, Brim would have rocked right back up on her. Cynthia had taken his young ass the distance.

Brim laid motionless with his eyes closed allowing his heart rate to return to normal. Cynthia tapped his leg getting his attention. When he opened his eyes, Cynthia was holding out the backwood that he pre-rolled and a book of matches. He took the items from her and blazed the backwood.

There's nothing like busting a good nut in the morning followed behind some good purp, Brim thought.

Cynthia stood between his legs brushing her teeth looking down at him with lust in her eyes. She looked sexy as fuck standing there naked with his Money Mafia chain on.

"You want breakfast?" Cynthia removed the toothbrush from her mouth and covered her mouth with her emptied hand. Brim nodded his head and watched Cynthia's booty bounced with every step when she departed the room.

Brim inhaled the purp deeply. His thoughts wandered back to last night on the roof of the buildings. He could relate to Shoota's pain. He felt everything Shoota said and going through. He understood the need for Shoota to be his own boss. He could relate to Shoota on making a sacrifice for Musa and not fully being rewarded for the sacrifice in fact the sacrifice made Brim suffer dearly. Brim blew out smoke and wondered should he have a talk with Shoota and let him know that he could relate to him and they were on the same page. Brim took another pull of the backwood and let the purp take him back to the time when he sacrificed it all for Musa.

***

6 ½ Years Ago

The summer night was like an oven. The smothering heat made sweat trickle down the small of Brim's back. He flipped the bottom of his black t-shirt and used it to wipe the sweat from his face.

The .38 special he had concealed in the front pocket of his jeans felt like it weighed fifty pounds. Brim stood in the darkness on the porch of an abandoned house. He watched the traffic flow of the smoke house that was resting directly across the street from where he was lurking.

One-Punch had been in the smoke house getting high for the last two hours. Brim couldn't wait until he came out because the night heat had all types of gnats flying around nd sticking to his sweaty skin. Snitching was never an option to Brim, especially when a muthafucka was out there in the streets living life as a savage and being a crackhead didn't give you a pass to be a rat.

One-Punch had Musa and Shoota sitting over D.C. jail fighting for their freedom because he'd fingered Musa as the person who shot him. Shoota didn't do shit to One-Punch but since he was in the car with Musa immediately after shooting when the police pulled Musa's car over it made him an accomplice.

What added insult to the situation was that One-Punch and Fat Corey tried to rob Musa for fourteen grams of coke. The robbery failed when Musa upped his fire and let off a few shots. Musa thought he had missed One-Punch and Fat Corey, but he was wrong, One-Punch was hit in the ass.

When Musa hit Brim's line and conveyed the situation to him in code that One-Punch was a rat, he was more than eager to punish One-Punch. Brim always respected Musa and Shoota. They were the only ones to give him a chance to get money in the hood. So, he felt he was obligated to take the hit to show his loyalty to Musa. Soon as their Money Mafia crew was put together it quickly died because Musa went to jail. Brim felt that it was his duty to make a great effort to keep Money Mafia. He and Ace still sold coke in front of the Ledroit Park building, but most of that money went to Musa and Shoota's legal fees. Brim needed Musa home so he could continue getting money.

The only problem Brim had with killing One-Punch was the fact that One-Punch and Brim's mom had a special relationship. Brim's mom had beat the odds and recovered from crack. She didn't give credit to God for helping her overcome her addiction, she gave all the credit to One-Punch. Brim's mom loved One-Punch with every limb of her body. She confessed that she would never turn her back on One-Punch.

Brim felt that his mom could do better without One-Punch in her life. He hated that his mom loved a crackhead. Brim never knew what One-Punch did to get his mother clean all this was before for his time. All he knew was that One-Punch had to go.

The door opened to the smoke house, and One-Punch appeared from where Brim was standing. He could tell One-Punch was higher than the old-World Trade Centers.

Brim's senses became highly alerted. He removed the .38 special from his pocket and emerged from the shadows of darkness real quiet like a cat. One-Punch never saw the movement from the other side of the streets. The crack he'd been smoking for the last few hours had him zoned and his mind was preoccupied with the task of getting more of it. Brim was up on One-Punch quick like a thief in the night.

Brim wanted to follow One-Punch until he got to the opening of the alleyway before calling his name, "One-Punch!"

A startled One-Punch pivoted around ready to throw his signature punch, but he quickly lowered his guard when he saw Brim behind him, calling his name.

"What's up, Brim?" One-Punch asked looking around the darkness of Keefer Street

"Musa said since you can't hold your tongue hold these," Brim replied, upping the .38 special.

Boom! Boom! Boom! Boom! Boom! Boom!

Brim emptied the gun cylinder and put four bullets in One-Punch's chest and two in his head. Brim hit the alleyway and disappeared into the night.

A week later Brim's mother was getting ready to attend One-Punch's funeral and she begged Brim to attend, but he refused.

"Brimain, come here for a minute let me talk to you," Brim's mom called from her bedroom.

Brim was rolling a blunt, he was about to blaze and meet with Ace to head downtown and attend Musa's and Shoota's court hearing.

"Alright, ma, I'm coming." Brim quickly finished twisting the blunt, put his stash of weed up and made it to his mother's room.

She was sitting on the bed, patiently waiting for him, he knew that his mom was taking the loss of One-Punch hard. He felt like shit knowing he was the cause behind her pain. His mother had cried herself to sleep every night after finding out One-Punch was murdered. Helene's eyes were puffy and red. Brim could tell she'd been recently crying and his heart ached.

"Wassup, Ma," Brim said, kissing her forehead, and taking a seat next to her on the bed.

Helene grabbed her son's hands and looked into his eyes. She cleared her throat. "One-Punch may not have been a good man in your eyes."

"Come on, Ma, you called me in here for this?" Brim asked, getting annoyed.

"Baby, just give me a chance to explain. You at least owe me and One-Punch that much," Helene stated firmly. Brim said nothing, he just lowered his head and stared at the back of him mom's hands that still gripped his. "You once asked me what I saw in One-Punch? I've been knowing One-Punch forever. We used to pull moves together and we got high together."

The thought of his mother getting high bothered Brim. He had seen what a real crackhead looked like first-hand and the thought of his mom being that hurt him.

"After having you, I was strung out on drugs real bad. I had no control no will power. You being an infant and needing to be constantly cared for was outta my means of doing." Tears of pain dripped down Helene's face. Brim squeezed his mom's hand tight. Helene wiped her tears away and continued, "I didn't know no one that wanted a crack baby."

Brim lifted his head at his mom's words. He never knew he was born with an addiction. Brim had so many questions, but he wanted to hear his mom out.

"I was at my end. I couldn't take care of you and continue to smoke crack. So, one day I made up my mind to get rid of you and submit to my crack addiction. I put you in the microwave and set the timer for ten minutes."

Brim's heart raced in his chest and a mix of sorrow and anger overcame him, but he suppressed his anger. Helene studied her son's face, while tears continued to stream down her face. Brim look at his mom with pain in her eyes. The reality set in that his mom was going to cook him in a microwave because she was too strung out on crack to take care of him. The guiltiness he felt for taking One-Punch out of her life was no longer a factor to him. He still wanted to know what stopped his heartless mom from killing him.

"What stopped you, ma?" Birm asked in a whisper.

Helene cleared her throat and wiped her tears away with the palm of her hands. She took a deep breath and continued, "Before I could hit the start button. One-Punch appeared out of nowhere, snatched you out of the microwave and cradled you in his arms. One-Punch helped me get clean. He forced me into rehab. He took care of you for nine months while I completed rehab and got clean. He wanted a better life for me and you. That's why I'm so grateful for One-Punch. He saved me so I could save you. I know he wasn't the best of men but he was a good man. Your father loved you, Brim."

"Father! What you trying say, Ma? One-Punch was my pops?" Brim asked through tears.

"Yes, Brimain, One-Punch was your dad!"

***

"Brim, baby, the food is ready!" Cynthia yelled from the kitchen.

Brim was brought out of his flashback, he wiped tears from his eyes, and step in his boxers. The day Helene told Brim that One-Punch was his dad he never spoke another word to her. After One-Punch's funeral, Helene relapsed.

"All for the love of Money Mafia," Birm said to himself as he walked out of the bedroom to go see what Cynthia had cooked.

Jibril Williams

Chapter 11

Jassii walked into Jacob's hospital room blowing steam off the coffee she held in her hands to keep her hands warm. The A.C. in Howard University Hospital was pumping. No matter how many layers of clothes she put on she could not get warm. So, she decided a hot cup of coffee from the hospital cafeteria would her and her tingling cold hands.

Jassii went and checked on her brother. He was resting and recovering from a four-hour surgery. The doctors had to reconstruct the left side of Jacob's jaw, because it was badly broken. The doctors believe he was struck with a construction hammer. They came up with that conclusion based on the round circular markings that were left on his body, the markings were the markings that only a hammer could make.

The police also found a hammer on the floor in Jacob's bedroom, the hammer had blood on it. The police assumed the blood found on the hammer was Jacob's. They were running DNA tests on the hammer to determine if the blood was Jacob's or not. Jassii hadn't spoken to her brother yet. She didn't know who attacked her brother, but she was going to make it her business to find out. The doctors said Jacob was heavily sedated and when the meds wore off, he was going to wish he was still under sedation. Jassii stared down at what used to be her brother's handsome face.

Her cold hand touched the bandages covering Jacob's swollen face. Jacob was Jassii's only sibling, they were all each other had besides their seventy-five-year-old grandmother. Jassii didn't inform their grandmother of Jacob's situation. She was afraid if she would have told her, the news would cause the old woman to have a heart attack.

Before Jassii met Ace almost three years ago. She and Jacob played the low-key stick-up game. Jassii would dance at the club and meet all the outta town action who had the big bag. Jassii would lay a trap for them, and Jacob would relieve them of their valuables. Jassii had been hearing noise about Money Mafia and Musa. She found out that Ace was second in command of the street organization. Jassii's plan was to go after Musa, but once she found out Ace was into women, she and Jacob's plan changed. They had intentions of robbing Ace and Musa, but after Jassii got to know Ace, she fell in love with her, and she couldn't go through with the plan to rob Ace and Musa.

Jassii hated looking at her brother in his condition. Her eyes started filled with tears. She removed her hand from Jacob's face and took a seat next to the window. She just had to take her eyes off Jacob for a minute, she was tired of crying. Jassii thanked God that her brother was still breathing because whoever robbed Jacob could have easily killed him. The doctors said whoever did this had no intention to kill him because he had no direct head trauma.

Sitting down in a small, thin, cushioned chair, Jassii wiped her tears away and sipped her cup of coffee. She wanted badly to call Ace and have her come to the hospital to comfort her and help her through this situation. The pain and vision of Ace and Musa kissing wouldn't allow her to dial Ace's number.

Ace knows where I am and what I'm going through, Jassii thought.

She tightened her jaw and ran a cold hand through her hair. Every time Jassii closed her eyes she was hit with the image of Ace and Musa passionately kissing. Jassii immediately opened her eyes and more anger washed over her. Jassii had asked Ace numerous of times was there something between her and Musa. Ace always convinced her that she didn't have a thing for Musa. Ace always professed, Musa was her best friend and brother figure. Ace claimed Musa never tried to have sex with her but seeing Ace and Musa's real life tongue action told her that Ace had deceived her. Now Jassii didn't even feel bad about cheating on Ace with Shoota. Jassii's only concern now was that Ace felt the same pain she was feeling from her betrayal.

***

Slurp! Slurp! Slurp! Slurp!

"Damn, daddy, I been sucking it for about forty minutes you ain't cum yet? You not even into it. Your mind's somewhere else. My jaws hurt, Shoota!" Darnella whined.

Darnella was one of Shoota's jump offs. Shoota had been up all-night smoking, drinking and contemplating how he was gonna handle the situation with Musa. He called Darnella over to his duck off apartments and help get his mind off Musa. Darnella had been giving Shoota head since she walked through the door. Mentally Shoota wasn't in the room, even though his manhood was standing tall like a flagpole. Shoota's mind was in a dark place.

"What you say?" Shoota asked coming out his trance. "Don't stop," he instructed Darnella.

Darnella rolled her eyes. "No, Shoota, my jaws hurt. You're going to have a bitch with locked jaws in a minute if I keep going." Darnella pouted while slightly stroking Shoota's wood.

Darnella sat Indian style between Shoota's legs while he sat on the edge of the couch. Shoota's face balled up into anger.

"Bitch, get the fuck up!" Shoota snapped mushing Darnella's face. The force from the push had her tumbling over backward. Shoota jumped to his feet, dick swinging in the process.

Darnella was taken aback by Shoota's sudden actions. He'd never been violent toward her. It scared her but it also made her want to right her wrong.

"Okay, Shoota, let me try again. I'll try harder this time. I promise I will," Darnella begged.

"Hoe ass bitch, get your shit and get the fuck on." Shoota pulled up his pants and secured his manhood.

He dug in his pocket, pulled out a few hundreds and threw them on top of Darnella. She looked down at the money and back up at a raging Shoota. She knew it was in her best of interest to get her belongings and leave.

Darnella scraped the few bills off the floor with a bruised ego. She located her Michael Kors handbag. Shoota watched her every move. Darnella walked to the door and placed her hand on the doorknob.

She stopped and turned to face Shoota, tears cascaded down her face. Darnella stuck her middle finger up at Shoota before she walked out slamming the door behind her.

Shoota chuckled at Darnella's performance. He knew if he would have opened the door and called after Darnella she would have come back running. Shoota picked up the bottle of Hennessy, removed the bottle cork and took a gulp from the bottle. The all-night drinking had Shoota's taste buds spent. He couldn't even taste the cognac splashing against his tongue. Shoota sat on the ottoman that sat in front of the couch, his head hung low. His thoughts quickly turn to Musa.

How could the nigga be so ungrateful? How could he not see that I'm capable and worthy of becoming my own boss? My own man! My loyalty and my sacrifice mean nothing to Musa. How could that be? Shoota thought.

Nigga's always screaming they want loyalty, they need good, solid, stand-up niggas around them. But once they get them, they don't know how to appreciate the loyalty a person shows them. Money Mafia was supposed to be theirs, but somehow Money Mafia became Musa's and Ace's. Everyone else affiliated with the Money Mafia are just their workers. Shoota couldn't see himself being a slave to Musa, Ace or Money Mafia. It was clear that Musa wasn't going to let him leave and branch out on his own. Shoota had already established a small team in Baltimore. He just needed Musa to open up the pipeline for the Heroin to him.

If Musa wasn't going to see him as an equal, then it wasn't any reason to continue being loyal to Musa. Musa had already accused him of being on some snake shit. *If that's how Musa saw his childhood friend, the nigga that took a gun charge for him. A muthafucka that went to prison for him.* If a snake is how Musa viewed him.

Then a snake I'll be, Shoota silently thought.

Chapter 12

Bzzz! Bzzz! Bzzz!

The buzzing of Musa's phone brought him out of his deep slumber. The stressful day he had yesterday combined with the bottle of Patron he consumed had him wanting to disregard the vibrating phone that was shaking like it was having a seizure on the nightstand. Musa stretched his body in bed getting the sleep out of his stiff muscles before he rolled over and picked up the phone.

"Hello!" Musa said in a raspy voice caused by sleepiness. Musa didn't even check to see who was calling before he answered the phone.

"Musa Blackwell!"

Hearing his whole government name made Musa's eyes open instantly. "Who the fuck is this?" Musa asked, a little irritated.

"Yeah, it's been a while. We definitely have to get reacquainted. This is your parole officer, Mr. Braxton.

Musa sat up in bed. "Oh, wassup, Mr. Braxton?" Musa wiped the sleep out of the corners of his eyes. Musa must've sat up too fast because he could feel the light throb occur in the cerebrum of his brain. Musa knew it was the after-effects of drinking a bottle of Patron to the head.

"A few things are up but nothing to be alarmed about. I need you to report to my office so we can have a face-to-face update. It's been over eight months since you visited my office. So, let's set a date for the day after tomorrow. How does that sound, Mr. Blackwell?"

Musa was hesitant to confirm if he was coming in for a face-to-face meeting with his parole officer. So much shit was running through Musa's head, and one was giving dirty urine.

Musa cleared his throat, "Umm, Mr. Braxton, will you be requesting a urine sample from me when I come to our office?" Musa asked.

There was silence over the phone before Musa parole officer spoke, "A urine sample won't be necessary, Mr. Blackwell. You coming to see me is all update and paper purposes. I'm trying to determine if I can remove you from parole early."

Musa hearing this let out a sigh of relief, but he still had an unsettling feeling in his gut. Musa just chalked it up as side-effects from last night Patron.

"Okay, I will be there. What time?" Musa asked

"You seem a little skeptical, Mr. Blackwell. I tell you what pick me up in front of the parole office building at 10:30 in the morning the day after tomorrow. Make sure you drive the Taycan. I never rode in a Porsche before," Mr. Braxton stated and laughed into the phone.

Musa antennas went up. The Porsche was one of his newest cars to his connection. He hadn't been driving the Porsche around the city like he had with the Maserati or the Audi truck. Now meeting up with parole officer in his Taycan made him more curious as well as cautious.

"Alright, Mr. Braxton, I will see you then," Musa agreed.

"Okay, great see you then, Musa," Mr. Braxton stated hanging up before Musa could reply.

Musa hit the phone icon button and laid the phone back on the nightstand. He planted his feet on the smoke gray plush carpet. He was trying to wrap his mind aground the call from the parole officer. Mr. Braxton mentioned the Porsche he had and the way he called him by his first name had Musa wondering. Musa rubbed his hands over his face. The thumping in his head was getting worse as he thought harder about the strange call. Mr. Braxton became Musa's parole officer 3 ½ years ago when he was release from prison after doing a three to nine bid for possession of fourteen grams of crack that he got caught with the night he shot One-Punch in his ass.

One-Punch ended up meeting an early demise which cause Musa and Shoota's attempted murder charges to be dropped. Shoota pleaded to the gun and Musa wore the crack charge. He was sentenced to three to nine years in prison. Musa did three years flat and was granted parole the first time seeing the parole board. Musa was assigned to Mr. Braxton's caseload. Mr. Braxton was laid back. He allowed Musa to do him. He gave Musa the impression that every man that came in front had a fair shake. Mr. Braxton explained that every man had a chance to do right or wrong. It wasn't his place to govern you, but only to make sure your transition back to society was a smooth one.

Mr. Braxton allowed Musa to work where he wanted as long as he provided a monthly pay stub and piss clean. Once Musa opened his own electronic warehouse business, Mr. Braxton praised him for doing good and encouraged him to continue to make smart choices. The only concern Mr. Braxton had about Musa's new business was where the money came from to start his business. Musa produced a contract of agreement for Ace and him to start a business together and open Acez Electronics. Musa showed where Ace received a small business loan from Bank of America for a $25,000 loan to start their business. Mr. Braxton reviewed the documents and was okay with the deal. Mr. Braxton has been very hands off with Musa and with that Musa started to push Mr. Braxton to the back of his mind.

The pain in Musa's head was started to really pound. He was in the process of lying back down when his phone vibrated again on the nightstand. Musa aggressively snatched the iPhone up and saw that it was Ace calling. He was going to ignore the call but thought against it thinking something may be going on.

"Wassup, Ace?" Musa said, lying back on the bed and closing his eyes.

"How you feeling?" Ace replied.

"Trying to pull myself together. I got a helluva hangover. My head killing me."

"Ummm! You need some help with that head?" Ace moaned which made Musa's eyes pop open.

"What you say, Ace?"

"Oh, do yo need me to bring you something for your headache?"

"Nah, I'm good. I'll be even better once I take another shot of Patron and put something on my stomach." Musa let out a deep breath.

"That's what got you that crucial hangover, that Patron! Are you sure you want to dance with the devil again so early in the morning?"

"The quickest way to get over a hangover is another shot of what you was drinking the night before," Musa mumbled.

"Can we talk about last night?" Ace asked changing the subject this was her real motive behind calling Musa so early in the morning. She been up all-night thinking, crying, and fantasizing about Musa and their possibilities.

"What about last night, Ace?" Musa inquired nonchalantly like he had no clue what Ace was talking about. A stillness fell over the phone. Ace let out a deep breath. "I'm talking about the passionate kiss we shared, Musa."

Just as quick as a storm suddenly appeared out of nowhere. The kiss he shared with Ace shine bright like a prism in his mind. He felt that same passion Ace was talking about. He couldn't deny it and he was glad Ace chose to call him and have this discussion rather than have this talk with him in person. If Ace would have chosen the latter, she would have been there to witness his manhood pressing against the fabric of his Gucci boxer briefs. The thought of kissing Ace's soft lips stirred something within him, but he would never admit it.

"Come on, Ace, you know the Patron we was drinking had us crossin' all the wrong lines," Musa's statement made Ace mad.

"I can't believe you're going to sit on the other end of this damn phone and act like Jamie Fox and blame it on the alcohol. What's all the wrong lines we crossed, Musa? We are fucking grown."

"Ace, you need to get your emotions in check," Musa said. Ace's added to the pounding in his head.

"Musa, are you saying you didn't feel nothing in the kiss that we shared?" Ace asked

"Nothing but a wet tongue."

"You are bogus as fuck right now, Musa!" Ace screamed into Musa's ear making him quickly remove the phone away. He placed the phone on speaker and laid the phone in his chest.

"Why you trying to force something that's not really there? You like my fucking sister. Ain't you supposed to be gay or some shit like that?" Musa was callous with his words.

Ace let that shit go. It was something that never should have happen.

"Let it go." Musa was started to get aggravated about the situation. "Ace, I don't need a relationship. I need a solid business partner. Someone I can trust. Can I count on you to be that person?" Musa asked.

Ace paused, she wasn't sure what choice of words she was going to use. "I got you, Musa. You can always count on me. My bad for stepping out of line but you know my feelings run deep for you," Ace stated calmly and disconnected the call, not giving Musa a chance to reply.

Musa disconnected the call also. He knew his words had hurt Ace, but he could not allow himself to engage in a relationship with Ace. He didn't know why but it had been like that since they met. He found Ace attractive and at times he would check her assets out when she wasn't looking. The voice in his head always screamed, *"No!"* When he thought about sexing Ace.

So, he listened to his instincts. Musa tried to clear him mind, but with the thumping headache and the morning drama with Ace and Mr. Braxton there was no clearing it. He got up to handle his handover and then to handle his daily business as Money Mafia's boss.

Jibril Williams

Chapter 13

Ace sat Indian style on her California bed. Her feelings were crushed. She stayed up all night convincing herself that Musa had finally come to his senses and seen the woman in her, but she was rejected by the only man that she ever loved. The fact that Musa didn't view her in that manner crushed her. Ace felt like a complete fool to even think Musa would see her as more than a friend or someone that he got the bag with. Ace wiped the falling tears from her face, so many emotions ran through her. Ace couldn't comprehend what was so wrong with her that Musa wouldn't choose her to be his woman.

She'd been so loyal to him to a tee. When Shoota and Musa went to jail she was the one that got knee deep in the streets and grinded with Brim to get rid of the remaining kilos. She spent months serving nickel bags hand to hand for Musa so he could have a decent lawyer. She did that so Musa didn't have to worry about commissary and money for phone calls. When the product ran out. She did something that few women would have, that had a nigga they was rocking with that was in jail. Ace paid Brim his earnings of the money from the product, she shut shop down and got her a job at Mazza Gallery on Wisconsin Avenue. She'd saved every dime they made from the kilos, with the money she made from her job she paid her bills.

Ace did all those things to try and win Musa over to show him that she was worthy of being his woman. Thinking about these things made Ace angrier. She balled up her fists and squeezed tight. Ace just couldn't understand why Musa didn't want her. The realization of her never being Musa's lover rocked her core. Ace had always been in love with Musa from the first day she met him. She laid down on her bed and allow her mind to take a trip down memory lane.

Ace had always been into females since she was nine years old. For this very reason, her father disowned her. It seemed that Ace's lust for the same sex got her into more trouble and today was no different. Ace had been creeping with the school dyke's girlfriend.

Somehow the word got back to the dyke who was known as Bam. Instead of Bam whipping her girlfriend's ass for cheating on her. She chose to whip Ace's ass instead.

"Bitch, you creeping with mine!" Bam asked before she punched Ace square in the forehead it was like the mule had kicked Ace.

Ace saw all types of lights and stars from the punch. Ace knew she couldn't fight the mammoth of a woman. Bam outweighed Ace by a hundred pounds. The bitch looked like Rick Ross without the beard. Ace tried to stand her ground, she went into fight mode, swinging her arms in a windmill motion with her fists balled up. Ace connected a few punches to Bam's face but that only motivated the crowd of spectators to sound off with their Ooooo's which only enraged the brute woman further.

Bam threw a meaty right hook that hit Ace in the jaw dropping her to the warm concrete. Ace could feel the concrete biting into her skin. She was mad dizzy and breathing hard. Bam kicked her in the stomach knocking the wind out of Ace, forcing her to see stars and knocking the breath out of her.

Ace knew she didn't have a chance to win the fight. She rolled over on her back desperately fighting to get some oxygen in her lungs. Ace looked up from the ground into Bam's eyes. Bam looked down at Ace and the coldest look ever came into focus of Bam's eyes. She spit on Ace and she raised her high-top Air Force Ones in the air over top of Ace's head. Just before Bam could bring her size 12 boy's shoe down on her pretty face she was brutally pushed to the ground.

"Bitch, what the fuck you doing? You way too big to be bumping with shorty!" Musa yelled with his face scrunched up.

Bam looked up at Musa from the ground like she wanted to jump and try a round or two with him. The push to the ground made the skin on Bam's elbow rip. The crowd around the fight grew quiet. The Rick Ross looking chick climbed to her feet with hate in her eyes, but she didn't dare say shit to Musa.

She addressed Ace though, "Stay the fuck away from my bitch." Bam walked off, picking the shredded loose skin from her elbow.

*Ace didn't even hear the dyke's threats; she was too busy star-
ing into Musa's grey eyes. The energy radiating off Musa had Ace
feeling a type of way. Even though she got her ass whipped and was
banged up, she still could feel the heat and the moisture come to life
in between her thighs. Ace's body had never did this over a man. "
You a'ight, slim?" Musa asked as he helped Ace off the ground.
Ace couldn't break eye contact with Musa. She was at a loss for
words. So, all she could do was nod, her twelve-year-old heart was
racing in her chest.
Bzzz! Bzzz! Bzzz!*

Ace's vibrating phone brought her back to her present state. She
reluctantly picked up the one resting next to her on the bed. She had
a notification that someone had sent her a video. The video was
from Jassii. Ace rolled her eyes in annoyance. She didn't want to
deal with Jassii right now. She knew Jassii was going to have tons
of questions about her and Musa kissing.

Ace assumed the video was one of many videos they had made
together when they ventured off to some exotic place. Ace thought
Jassii had sent her the video to remind her of what they had together

Ace didn't want to view none of their happy times. She just
wanted to clear her head and get her emotions in check about Musa.
What she was feeling was a ball of confusion. A part of her loved
Musa like a brother but she wanted him intimately like a husband.
The other half of her was upset that Musa rejected her. It was too
much for her little heart to bear. On top of that she still had feelings
for Jassii and she had to deal with the fact she had hurted Jassii and
betrayed her trust.

Ace didn't play the video. She laid the phone next to her, closed
her eyes and took a deep breath. She needed to unwind and relieve
some stress. Ace was trying to do that when she called Musa to talk
about what transpired between them last night. Before she called
Musa, she was lying in bed, legs open, massaging her clit thinking
about how soft Musa's lips felt on hers. She needed to hear Musa's
voice to get her where she needed to be. Ace thought Musa may
have caught onto her sexual undertones when she asked him if he
needed help with that head.

Ace was almost at her peak when Musa rejected her. Her orgasm washed away like tides, washing away writings in the sand. Ace got out of bed and hoped that a hot shower would take some stress away. Twenty minutes later, Ace was out of the shower feeling a little better. She made up her mind that she was going to call Jassii, apologize to her, find out what hospital she was at with her brother and go sit with her. She wasn't worried about Jacob telling Jassii that Brim and her was the ones who fucked him over. Ace was going to play the loving supporting girlfriend.

Ace sat down on the bed and gave her Amazon echo commands to play *Trey Songz* album *Back Home*. She started the task of twisting some loud pack in a cherry flavor backwood. When she felt the vibration of her phone on the bed. Ace reached for the phone and saw that it was a text from Jassii. Ace put fire to the backwood that was now hanging from her lips. She took a few pulls off the wood before reading Jassii text.

//: *U not the only one who can get some dick. Hope U like the video as much as I liked making it!*

Ace's face scrunched up when she read the text. Ace immediately went to the video and hit play on her screen. The video came into focus and Ace's heart broke into a thousand pieces. She watched her lover's head go up and down on the thickest piece of manwood she'd ever seen.

Jassii seemed to be enjoying performing oral on whoever she was performing it on. Ace couldn't see the nigga's face. It was confirmed that Jassii was enjoying herself when she popped dude's dick out of her mouth and asked him did he like it. Ace watched the video five times while she smoked her backwood. When she was done, Ace felt like she wanted to die.

Chapter 14

Brim got into Shoota's G-Wagon. "What's good, slim?" Brim said as he dapped Shoota.

"This paper!" was Shoota's only words.

Brim noticed Shoota didn't hit him with his normal greeting when he was asked, *"What's good?"* Any other time Shoota would be screaming, *"Money Mafia all day every day."* Brim noticed that Shoota's vibe was off and dark, but that was expected due to the events that transpired between them yesterday.

Shoota pulled away from the curb of Brim's crib. Brim had just gotten home about an hour ago from fucking Cynthia all night. He was tired as fuck. All he had enough time to do was shower and feed his two pitbulls before Shoota hit him saying that he was on his way to scoop him so they could make their two-week drop off in Alexandria.

They rode in silence listening to Money Baggs before Brim made up his mind to break quell in the truck. "I don't think what Musa did was boss."

Shoota didn't saying nothing to Brim's statement, he just drove stone-faced with his eyes playing the G-wagon mirrors. Brim didn't know how Shoota was going to respond to his statement.

"Everything that nigga did yesterday wasn't kosher, slim." Shoota took his eyes briefly off the road and looked at Brim. They were headed toward 14th Street Bridge. "Musa didn't even have enough respect for me to hear me out and see things from my point of view." Shoota shook his head in dismay.

"Every man wants to be his own boss nobody should work under another forever."

"True word of a nigga that feels my struggle," Shoota said glimpsing into his rearview mirror. He pushed the truck to the bridge going 55 mph. "It's like Musa ain't respecting my mind as a man."

"Or your gangsta!" Brim chimed in.

Shoota quickly looked over at Brim like he was trying to read his expression to see if Brim's statement had some hidden words behind them. Shoota placed his eyes back on the road. Brim felt the instant awkwardness in the truck right after the words left his mouth.

His pulse quickened. "Slim, I didn't mean shit by what I just said, but you know I'm a realest. Life gives you what you see. That's what's wrong with our people. They see life through the lens of illusion instead of seeing things for what they are and what they are worth."

Shoota just kept driving. He wanted to hear Brim's thoughts on life and his current situation. "How you figure that?" Shoota asked, trying to keep the young goon talking.

"It's like this—muthafuckas play lotto trying to get rich but they know the chances of them winning is slim to none but they keep playing trying to win while those who control the lotto continue to get rich off other's desires to get rich. It's an illusion that lotto people have created. We keep playing lotto hoping to get rich."

"So, what you saying is that Musa has created an illusion for us with Money Mafia? We all getting rich off Money Mafia so you can't compare lotto to Money Mafia," Shoota retorted.

"Money has nothing to do with the Money Mafia because the Mafia has always been about money. In our situation, it's about status, about us being our own bosses, having our own Money Mafia. It's Musa that's living the illusion. He's living the illusion that he's the only boss. That's why he would never see the bosses in us. It never came across his mind that one day we may want to run our own organizations." Shoota nodded in agreement.

"So, how do we get Musa to see things from our perspective?"

Now it was Brim's turn to search Shoota's face for any sign that his words held something hidden behind them.

"Bruh, the hardest thing ever is to get someone to see outside of their own illusion. All we can do is talk with Musa and if that don't work, we have two options. Stack paper, relocate and start over from nothing or continue to work under Musa and Ace," Brim said looking out over the water that flowed under the 14th Street Bridge.

"For a minute there I thought you was gonna say we had to pop Musa and take over," Shoota said

"Man, you thinking reckless. Friends don't murder friends this violates Money Mafia's bylaws."

"Good response, slim," Shoota said, turning Money Baggs up. His hands were sweaty, he was close to revealing to Brim what he had on his mind. Shoota's phone rang it was Musa. He didn't want to answer but he did anyway, "Yeah!" Shoota stated dryly.

"Where your location?"

"Heading out VA to handle that little business we got popping off every two weeks. Why, what's up?"

"Say less just come through the crib later tonight so we can talk," Musa said

"Aye, Mu, if this about yesterday—"

"Shoota, just come through," Musa said, cutting him off and disconnecting the call.

Shoota looked at Brim and Brim shrugged like he didn't have a clue why Musa wanted to see him at his crib. Shoota planted the seed in his mind that this could be the opportunity he was looking for. Shoota's phone vibrated in his lap. It was a text from Jassii notifying him that she sent Ace the video of her sucking his dick.

He shook his head and thought, *Bitches and their scandalous ways.*

***

Jassii turned her phone off and laid it on the tray cart that stood next to her chair. She rested her back on the back of the chair and closed her eyes. She'd just sent Shoota a text letting him know she revealed their little secret by sending Ace the video of her sucking his dick. Jassii smirked thinking about the mental anguish Ace was going through after she reviewed the video. Jassii knew that the video had affected Ace tremendously because Ace had been blowing up her phone with voicemails and texts, asking how she could betray their trust.

Ace went from that of a grieving girlfriend to she was going to beat her ass when she saw her in the streets. Jassii wasn't worrying about Ace's threats. All that was on her mind was her brother getting better and her winning the heart of Shoota.

Jibril Williams

Chapter 15

Sussex Square Apartments on Brooks Drive in Capitol Heights Maryland was Ace's second home. Ace shifted the Porsche into neutral and pulled back on the emergency brakes. She checked her eyes in the mirrors, bloodshot and teary eyes stared back at her. The reality of Jassii stealing thirty thousand dollars and cheating on her was too much to bear. Even though she was fighting an emotional war within herself, she was still undeniably in love with Musa. However, with Musa rejecting her that just added to the confusion that her heart and mind was suffering. She needed someone to talk to. It was times like these that she wished her mother was still alive.

Ace needed someone to help sort her problems out, that would listen to her and give her advice. Her mother was deceased, but Musa's mom wasn't and his mom was the closest thing she had to a mom. So, that was her reason for pulling up at mama Cheryl's crib.

Ace grabbed the two designer shopping bags off the passenger seat and climbed out of the Porsche. The Porsche doors locked on their own. Even though Ace was an emotional wreck her appearance was immaculate. The money green Louis Vuitton red bottoms had her standing sexy in her black Louis Vuitton jeans which appeared to be painted on her skin. The money green V-neck t-shirt matched with the red bottoms perfectly. The V-neck shirt bared a LV on the front, the added flavor to her fit was how she had the end of her bone straight ponytail dyed money green.

Ace used her small knuckles to knock on Musa's mom's door. She could hear music playing on the other side. Ace could hear *Anita Baker's* sweet melodic voice singing *Sweet Love*. It was something about the singer's words that made her cringe hearing the words, "Sweet Love!" Her eyes started to mist over. Ace thought maybe Ms. Cheryl didn't hear her knock. She was having second thoughts about coming to Ms. Cheryl's crib especially unannounced. She thought she'd just leave the bags at the door and call Cheryl when she got in the car and let her know she had a gift at her door, but before she could sit the bags on the floor, the door to Cheryl's apartment swung open and there stood her second mom.

"Ace!" Cheryl screamed and snatched Ace into her arms giving her a motherly hug.

Ace desperately needed a hug that was loaded with so much love. Ace squeezed Cheryl's back tightly. Being a mom Cheryl could feel Ace's hunger for a hug.

She waited patiently for Ace to release her before she cupped Ace face in her hands. "What's the matter, baby?"

"Is it that obvious?" Ace asked with a shy grin. Cheryl nodded searching Ace's familiar eyes. "Well, at least let me in first. I got gifts," Ace said, holding up the designer bags.

Cheryl's eyes got big. "Oh, no you didn't!" Cheryl pulled Ace inside the apartment, locked the door and took the bags from Ace. She waved Ace to sit down on the chocolate-colored leather couch. Cheryl sat next to her and opened the bag, removing a shoe box that held pink Christian Dior red bottoms and the second bag held a matching clutch purse. Ace swung by Wisconsin Avenue out Chevy Chase Maryland the Rodeo Drive of the East Coast and grabbed Ms. Cheryl a small token of her love.

"Oh, I'm gonna be the flyest MFer at NA tomorrow night," Cheryl said smiling.

Cheryl had been clean for years now, but she still attended NA because she knew addiction was a lifelong battle so she attended her 12-Step Narcotics Anonymous meeting twice a week to remind her that she had a daily fight on her hands and she needed help fighting her demons.

Cheryl was a tiny woman that stood 5'5 and wore 140- pounds. You could tell years of drug abuse had stolen some of her beauty, but she was still pretty. Her dark skin showed her deep African roots. Cheryl had a charming smile and didn't take no bullshit. She always spoke and told what was on her mind, even if it hurt your feelings or not.

"Thank you, baby. I swear between you and that damn son of mine, y'all gonna spoil me rotten," Cheryl said as she leaned over and gave Ace a hug for the second time today. Cheryl sat down next to Ace and placed Ace's hand into hers. "Now tell mama what's wrong?" Cheryl asked with care and interest in her voice.

Ace's eyes watered over, instantly put her head down and focused her eyes on she and mama Cheryl's hand. She was embarrassed to even tell Mama Cheryl what happened between Jassii and her. She didn't even know how to begin to convey how she felt about Musa. Cheryl waited patiently for Ace to speak. Cheryl could tell that whatever was bothering Ace had her emotions raw.

She removed her hand from Ace, placed it under Ace's chin and lifted it. "Ace, baby, never hold your head down unless you are praying or giving your lover some head."

This made both women share a laugh together breaking the sadness in Ace's heart.

Ace wiped her tears away and took a deep breath. "Mama Cheryl, I'm in love with Musa," Ace mumbled putting her head back down.

Mama Cheryl lifted her head right back up. A broad smile fell on Mama Cheryl's face. "Ace, you been in love with Musa ever since the first day he brought you to meet me after that dyke beat your ass at school. But it's good to finally hear you admit it. Now, how are we gonna tell Musa you are in love with him? You know you've always been my daughter-in-law," Cheryl stated ranting on.

Ace started crying more, that's when Cheryl knew there was more to the story. Let me guess, Ace, you're still in love with that fast ass girl Jassii?" Cheryl asked. Ace shook her head. "So, what's the problem Ace? What am I missing, baby?"

"I—well, me and Musa shared a kiss last night, but when I called him this morning to tell him how I felt, he rejected me. He made me feel that this kiss we shared was nothing, just another kiss that he shared with random bitches," Ace stated through tears. She wiped the dribbling snot from her nose with the back of her hand.

"Did my son say this to you or is this something you're assuming?" Cheryl inquired.

"I asked him did he feel the same connection that I felt in the kiss we shared. And he stated he felt nothing but a wet tongue."

Mama Cheryl's forehead creased, now she understood why Ace was feeling how she was. How Musa handled the situation had her wanting to kick her son's ass. She told Musa many times that Ace loved him and he should partake in her love and never take advantage of Ace's feelings. Musa always promised he would never hurt Ace. Cheryl was biased to the situation because she'd always been a fan of Musa and Ace hooking up and being a couple. She wanted to remain neutral in the situation because whether Musa and Ace got together or not. Ace would always be the daughter she never had and Musa or no one was going to change that.

"I don't know what's wrong with me, Mama Cheryl? What's so mess up about me that he won't chose me as his woman?"

"Don't you dare blame yourself for this. This is all on my son. There's nothing wrong with you, baby. My rock head son's Gucci shades must be too dark to see the gift he has in you."

"Oh, he sees the gift in me. I'm only qualified to be his business partner," Ace said sadly

It hurt Mama Cheryl's heart to hear those words. She knew there was some truth to those words. A few months ago, she was trying to convince Musa to pursue Ace and he'd told her he only saw Ace as a business partner or a sister type. Cheryl couldn't believe he was so callous to tell Ace those words to her face.

If this were any other person besides Ace, Cheryl wouldn't involve herself in her son's affairs. She would have advised Ace with the words, "Fuck Musa!" and "The best way to get over a man was to get under a new one." But she couldn't give Ace them words. She could see the love and hurt burning in Musa's eyes at the same time. "Ace you know your worth, so know that you are more than a business partner to my son. Don't even start believing that bullshit my son is feeding you. Keep pursuing his love. Love conquers all. He will come around, baby."

"You think so, ma?" Ace asked with still teary eyes. She wasn't expecting Mama Cheryl to give her the words that she did. Cheryl nodded. "But I think I done tried everything I can think of to convince Musa I'm worthy of being his queen."

"Well, have you thought about retiring from being his business partner? I mean he's saying that's all he sees you as. Why don't you retire and remove yourself as his business partner and maybe then he will see you as something else."

"I don't know about that, Mama Cheryl," Ace said but her mind was running a hundred mile an hour flipping over Mama Cheryl's advice and the more the idea did cartwheels in her head she could see the plan coming together.

Cheryl knew she was way out of pocket giving Ace the advice she did, but she was also hoping Musa would retire out of the drug game. Cheryl had a hidden agenda. She wanted Musa off the streets. If Ace got out of the game maybe Musa would follow her and view and see Ace in a different light. She knew Musa had plenty of money. She wanted her son out of the drug business while he had his life and freedom. She knew if Musa stayed out there in them streets long enough death, or a prison sentence would claim his life.

"Mama Cheryl, let me think about it—" The sound of keys turning in Cheryl's front door locks stopped Ace from talking.

Musa walked in looking sexier than a Chippendale dancer. Ace lowered her head and tried to will away the wetness that oozed between her legs.

"What's up, Ma!" Musa said, walking into his mother's crib.

"Not a damn thing," Cheryl stated flatly her response had Musa taken aback, but he ignored her because he already knew Ace was over his mom's crib putting her in his business and his Ma had already chosen her side. He made a note to check Ace's ass later.

"Ace you good?" Musa asked

"I'm perfect," she mumbled.

Musa wasn't for the bullshit. He was hungry, he was getting over his hangover and he was starving. He'd came past his mom's crib to check on her and get his eat on. All that extra shit Ace was on with her emotions rolled off him like water rolls off a duck's back. So, he paid no attention to Ace's nonchalant response to his greetings.

"Ma, I know that you cooked something. What you got cooking up in this camp?"

"Boy, I didn't cook nothing today. If your butt would have called before you came, I would have put something on for you," Cheryl said with a little irritation in her voice.

She was pissed at Musa at how he treated Ace. She was gonna dig in his shit the first chance she got when Ace wasn't around.

"Come on, Ma! I got to call first before I can get a home cooked meal," Musa complained walking into the kitchen and checking his Ma's fridge for some leftovers. Musa broke his face down into a frow. The fridge was full of food but there wasn't a leftover in sight. "Ma, where's the leftovers?"

"There's no leftovers, I threw them out yesterday." Cheryl stated.

She and Ace sat in the living room quietly with an awkward silence. They wanted Musa ass to leave so they could finish talking.

"If you want something to eat you gonna have to go get it because I'm not cooking until me and Ace get through talking. I don't know how long we'll be. Oh, but there is something on top of the fridge for you."

Musa looked on top of the fridge and removed a small white envelope that was addressed to him. He read the name of the sender and his heart raced with anger. "What the fuck this nigga want?" Musa barked from the kitchen

"Musa, watch your damn mouth!" Cheryl yelled.

Ace sat next to Cheryl wondering what was going on. To hear the distaste in Musa's voice made her ready to boot up and stand by Musa.

Musa came flying out of the kitchen with the letter in his hand. "Ma, what this nigga want? And how did he get this address. Have you talked with him?" Musa shot question after question at his mother.

"I don't know how he got my address. He wrote me a letter as well."

Cheryl didn't want to have this conversation in front of Ace despite the girl was practically family. "My letter was full of apologies and regrets. I'm sure yours will be the same but read the letter and see what he has to say."

Musa looked at his mom and he could tell she was holding back on him. He didn't know why. He folded the small envelope, placed it in his back pocket and left out of the front door without saying goodbye to his mom or Ace.

"Mama Cheryl, what was all that about?" Ace asked with her voice full of concern.

"Awww, baby, that's not about nothing. Musa just got a letter from his father."

Jibril Williams

Chapter 16

Sitting behind the wheel of his Porsche Taycan the folded letter slightly shocked caused by his trembling hands, anger and anxiety. Musa stared down at his father's name on the envelope, *Moses Blackwell*. The name poked at him and gave him that uneasy feeling you get when someone violated your personal space and stuck their finger in your face.

It had been sixteen years since Musa had seen or heard from his dad. He'd spent all those years without the man whose name he shared. Musa was the Islamic for Moses. They both meant the same thing. Musa couldn't understand why his pops could just abandon him. He understood that things weren't on the up and up between his dad and mom due to her drug addiction, but what about him and their relationship. What was the reason for his dad turning his back on his only child?

When Musa was young his dad used to come around off and on to drop Musa mom off a few dollars and give Musa some father and son quality time. Through some of Cheryl's get high buddies, Musa learned that he was a vicious stick-up artist and that was why Moses wasn't around much because his pops didn't want to bring any heat or danger to his mom and him. So, he stayed on the move.

Musa felt like this was bullshit though when he asked his mom about the things her friends told him about his dad when she wasn't around. Cheryl would tell him to stay outta grown folks business. She informed him that his dad really did love him but Musa felt otherwise because he'd spent many nights licking the crumbs out of the empty bread bags that were left in the kitchen. Too many days he was dizzy from lack of food to nourish his small body. Too many school days he had to be subject to bullying because he had hand-me-down shoes that his mama got from one of her crack smoking friends. Most of the hand-me-down shoes automatically came with holes in the bottom of them which he had to cover up with cardboard.

Musa blamed these things on his father. He didn't blame his mom too much for his living condition because he knew her drug use had her sick mentally. His dad on the other hand, got no passes to why they were so poor and why he had to live so harsh. Musa felt like his dad should have been his hero for him and his mom.

The last time Musa had seen or heard from his dad he was eleven-years old. Moses came past his mother's crib and hit her off with a wad of cash and took him shopping. His dad brought him everything he wanted that day. Musa had two pairs of Jordans and a pair of Timberland boots. His dad brought him twelve pairs of jeans, sweatsuits, new socks and drawers. Young Musa was so happy he never had that many clothes and shoes at the same time. He couldn't wait to show up at school to talk shit to the other kids who fucked with him about his rags and hole filled shoes.

After sliding past America's Best Wing to let Musa pig out on 50 pieces of the restaurant's best wings. Moses stopped pass Klassie Kutz barbershop on Alabama Avenue Southeast to get Musa a fresh fade. This day was the highlight of Musa's young life. To spend time with his dad and go shopping for what he thought was top of the line gear. It wasn't nothing like what he was feeling. He sat back in his dad's truck on the passenger's side feeling sleepy from all the food he ate and the excitement he had just running through the mall with his dad.

They rode through the city listening to the music that pumped through the caddy speakers. Until they came to stop at a red brick building.

"Musa I'm going to run in here and see someone. I'm gonna need you to sit tight until I get back," Moses said, looking over at Musa.

Musa moved his head up and down. He watched his dad remove some bags out of the back of the truck and make his way in the building. He wondered who the bags were for, but he quickly dismissed it as grown folks business like his mom always said when he started questioning things that didn't concern him. Musa messed around with the radio removing the old school slow jams that his pops had playing. He stopped when he heard *50 Cent's In The Club* playing he snapped his fingers and rapped along with 50.

Money Mafia

A brown-skinned girl stormed out of the red brick building and took a sit on the first step and from where Musa was sitting he could tell she was crying for some strange reason Musa wanted to get out of the truck and console the little girl. He could tell she was a few years younger than him.

The girl must have felt his eyes burning a hole in her because she looked up to catch him staring. They both locked eyes. The girl's eyes was enchanting. Before Musa could build up the courage to get out of the truck to talk with the girl, Big Moses came out of the building empty handed. His dad's presence made the girl jump. Moses stopped and stared down at the little girl before he stormed to the truck and pulled off. Musa hadn't heard from his dad since that day.

So, he wondered why this nigga decided to reach out to him now. Had he heard that he was the king of the city and was reaching out for a handout. Musa flipped the letter over to its back and used one of his keys to rip open the letter. Musa unfolded the letter and began reading.

Dear Son,

I'm hoping that this brief notation finds you well. As for myself I'm playing the hand that life has dealt me. I know this letter may come to some surprise, and I know you may be full of questions, resentment and hurt when it comes to me. And you have every right to be!

Musa my son there are some things I must explain to you. These matters are gravely important. I need you to come visit me asap. Time is of the essence. Just so you know I really do love you.

Always Musa, Dad

Musa must have read the letter at least five times before he balled it up and littered his mom's parking lot with it. He couldn't believe that his dad had the nerve to be gone all those years and up and write him with no apology—without an explanation. He summoned him like a dog and he expect Musa to come running.

"Nah, fuck nigga!" Musa mumbled before backing the Taycan out of the parking space. He was on a mission to find a place to eat to silence the grumblings in his stomach.

Chapter 17

Kicking the Louie Vs off his feet and falling back on the plush leather couch, Brim puffed the burning backwood hanging between his lips. The all-night fuck session with Cynthia and the all-day trapping with Shoota was tiresome. So, coming home early to catch up on a few hours of sleep was right up his alley. Brim inhaled the purp harshly not wanting none of the good weed to escape. Brim loved smoking weed, it helped him think, he did some of his best thinking when he was blowing one to the dome like he was doing now. White chalky smoke creeped from between his lips. He took another drag from the backwood but this time he blew the smoke out of his nostrils.

Brim relaxed and his mind started to drift. One-Punch's face appeared in the center of his mind. He wondered how One-Punch would have been as a dad. He contemplated why his mom never told him that One-Punch was his biological father. He could understand why One-Punch didn't want him to know he was his father. No father should want his child to see them weak and strung out on drugs, but his mother should have told him whether One-Punch wanted him to know or not. Every child had a right to know who their parents were.

Maybe if his mother would have conveyed this important to him, One-Punch would probably still be alive, and he wouldn't have to live with the burden of having his father's blood on his hands. For that reason, Brim chose to cut ties with his moms. He blamed her as taking part in One-Punch's death because she kept the fact that One-Punch was his dad a secret. If he would have known, he would have found a different alternative to stop One-Punch from testifying against Musa and Shoota. Brim didn't condone snitching, but One-Punch was his father where his bloodline began. He could have easily relocated One-Punch until Musa's trial was over.

Brim hit the backwood again and continued thinking. Another reason why he'd stopped talking and going around his mom was the fact that he couldn't look her in the eyes knowing he'd killed someone so dear to her. Brim fought back tears.

***

Shoota sunk low in his AMG strolling through pictures on IG. He lifted his head in time from his iPhone to see Jassii walking through the hospital parking lot toward his Benz truck. Jassii had texted him and asked if he could pull up. Being as though he was posted up around Ledroit Park after he and Brim had dropped off the fire joints to the VA niggas.

He felt that it was no pressure to fall through Howard University hospital to see what Jassii had on her mind. He needed to see why she revealed the sex video to Ace. He was also hoping for a quick fuck session. The all-purple Givenchy outfit Jassii had on looked sexy. The sway of her firm hips and thighs made Shoota's mouth water and had him adjusting his manhood through his jeans.

I'll definitely give Jassii a pussy pounding in the back of my truck, He thought.

As Jassii got closer to the truck he could tell their meeting wasn't going to be one of those encounters. He could see that she had been crying and once she climbed aboard his truck the tear streaks on her cheeks were a testament that she had been crying.

"Did you know, Shoota?" Jassii asked as soon as the truck door closed.

Shoota wasn't sure what the fuck Jassii was talking about. His eyebrows creased. "Know what?"

"Know that Ace and that nigga Brim was the one that fucked my brother over and put him in the hospital. They beat him with a fuckin' hammer, Shoota!" Jassii's nose flared as she raised her voice. Tears formulate in her eyes.

Still confused, Shoota shook his head. "Nah, shorty don't know shit about that play," once the words departed his mouth, he remembered that her brother Jacob ran off with some work Ace fronted him. So, his guess was that Ace and Brim had caught up with him.

"Come on, Shoota, you had to know. Ace, Brim and you are peoples, you know everything that goes down with them and the Money Mafia."

"Bitch, what the fuck I say? I don't know shit about Ace and Brim fucking your brother over. Are you sure it was them? Because Brim isn't the type of nigga that would leave a nigga breathing after he done violated them." Shoota popped his knuckles on his right hand.

Jassii pinched the bridge of her nose and let out a deep sigh "I know it was them. My brother wrote everything down on a notepad and told me that Ace and Brim kidnapped him from our grandma's house. He told me Ace sent him a text from me as if it was me and had him meet her at our grandma's." Jassii lifted her head.

Shoota wanted to laugh but suppressed it.

Ace gained some clever points with him with the move she pulled on Jacob.

"So, now what? Your brother's gonna rat on Ace like a bitch?" Shoota asked, searching Jassii eyes for the truth.

"Nigga, what! Me and my brother from the Southside of this city. Being a rat isn't part of our DNA, but I'll tell you this though, we not letting this shit slide."

"And y'all telling me this to say what?" Shoota stated cutting Jassii off.

He didn't have time to be listening to Jassii going on about she's about that life. Shoota believed that action was louder than words.

"I'm telling you because I want to know where you stand? I already know you have no real love for Ace based on our past conversations and the fact that you've been fucking me behind her back."

"What you got on ya mind, Jassii?" Shoota asked, getting impatient. He leaned his seat back with the power button. He unbuttoned his pants and removed his limp member.

Jassii saw Shoota's deflated meat stick and licked her lips. She knew it was all on her to make it happen. She needed Shoota on her team. She reached over and took Shoota's member in her soft hands and commence to slowly stroking Shoota's manhood.

"I want to get my pound of flesh from Ace. Ace has over a million dollars stashed at her crib. I have the combo to the safe and all," Jassii said leaning over and popping Shoota's now semi- erect dick in her mouth and swirled her long tongue around his piece, causing Shoota's hammer to sprang to life.

"Shit!" Shoota mumbled.

"What you need me to—to do?" Shoota asked between ragged breathing.

Jassii's oral performance had him already ready to bust. She removed Shoota from her mouth with a slurping sound.

"I want you to set Ace up for my brother. Me and my brother want some get back. We want to fuck her over and kill her." Jassii worked her saliva on Shoota's now palpitating rod. She used her spit as a lubricant to jack Shoota's rod up and down, with every stroke she had Shoota's pole shining like a well polish marble statue. "If you can handle this Zaddi we go fifty-fifty on the money." Jassii leaned back over and swiped her tongue over Shoota's helmet a few times leaving behind spit to continue to lube his pipe.

Shoota was contemplating the money along with the fact that Musa was shitting on him and had Ace above him when the Money Mafia was concern. Shoota came up with the conclusion if he didn't move on the situation that he would forever be stuck under and Ace.

"Damn, Jassii!" Shoota mumbled arching his back in the truck seat.

Jassii worked her thumb around his helmet with the precum that now seeped from his rod.

"Yeah, I can put the play together and get Ace out the way." Shoota committed to make the ultimate betrayal against his own team.

Jassii immediately kicked off her shoes and removed her jeans revealing she wasn't wearing any panties. She straddled Shoota like she was about to take a ride on a 1200 Kawasaki. She grabbed Shoota's manhood and treated it like a credit card and swiped it between her creases.

"When all this is over, it's me and you, fuck everyone else," Jassii stated.

Shoota stared into Jassii's beautiful eyes, he was lost in their allurement. "Like Lucious and Cookie Lyon off Empire," Shoota mumbled. His eye rolled in the back of his head as Jassii eased down on him.

Jibril Williams

Chapter 18

"Musa, why do you choose to ignore the red flags? Many men in the past who have occupied the same position as you failed to see the enemy among them? You have been blessed that your enemy has revealed himself." Musa was tired of hearing that Shoota his childhood friend was a potential enemy.

Shoota and him had been going through some things but they would never be adversaries. The letter that his dad sent him and the fact that his plug was preaching to him irritated Musa.

"Papaya, no disrespect but I got this. Shoota is not a threat to me or this organization. I'm having Shoota meet me to discuss a few things. Once we have our sit down, I will inform you of the outcome.

"There is nothing to discuss, Musa. Dig a hole and put Shoota in it," Papaya said through the phone in a whisper.

"That won't be necessary. I think I got shit under control. Once again, no disrespect but Shoota is a brother. Never talk about causing him harm, always put some respect on his name when you bring his name up in my presence," Musa aggressively spoke through the phone.

A silence fell over the phone. Musa knew the old man hadn't hung up, he was on the other end of the phone processing Musa's tone and words.

"In this business, Musa—we trust nobody. We don't attach ourselves to nothing not even our loved ones. Do you know why, Musa?" Musa didn't answer, he just waited for Papaya to tell him. "Because all these things hinder us from progressing to the next level of the business. It stops us from possessing that next level of power. Don't allow Shoota to hinder you from growing into the next levels this business has to offer. Once again, my apologies for the delay in the shipment like I said before some unforeseeable events transpired but the shipment will be there the day after tomorrow." Papaya disconnected the call.

Musa tapped the phone icon to end the call and laid the phone on his lap. He closed his eyes and laid his head back on the leather couch. He knew Papaya was mad that he wasn't in agreeance with killing Shoota, but there was no way he was going to kill Shoota or allow anyone else to down his right-hand man.

He was going to have to talk with Shoota and give him his blessing. He was hoping Shoota would take him up on his offer. He couldn't really fault Shoota for wanting to be his own boss. Musa felt a tap on his leg. He opened his eyes to a 5'7 Goddess standing naked before him accompanied by her also naked friend who was standing an even five feet.

Musa admired Nai's body. She had a body that made you want to pray to it and thank God for it all at the same time. Nai didn't have any blemishes on her body, her melon sized breasts sat firmly over top of her flat stomach. Her slightly trimmed butt had its own style of beauty. Her light, chocolate-colored skin made his mouth water.

"We're bored, Musa. When's your friend gonna be here?" Nai asked.

Musa didn't reply right away. He just took in Nai and her friend Kelly's nakedness. Kelly didn't have what Nai had in the looks or body, but she was strap in the ass and thigh department. Nai was a chick Musa met at a Howard homecoming a few months ago. She had been one of the many chicks that sent Musa naked pictures but when she sent him the pictures of her kissing Kelly, he had to see what their head and pussy do. He had them come over to help break the tension with Shoota.

"He should be here in a minute. Why don't you and Kelly go hit the bar up and get nice and lit? Once my nigga gets here and we do some talking, we'll be back there to join you and Kelly."

"You promise?" Nai asked, placing her foot up on the couch.

She started rubbing her fingers between her creases. He saw how quick Nai's fingers glazed over with her juices it made him want to get straight to action and it didn't help that Kelly had popped one of Nai's breasts in her mouth. Musa smirked and adjusted his manhood in his jeans. The chiming of the doorbell brought the entertainment to a halt.

"Let me handle this business and I'll be with you soon." Musa watched as both women's ass cheeks gave themselves a round of applause as they walk out of the living room.

Musa went and got the door. Shoota stood there with a distant look in his eyes. He looked Shoota over, Shoota's head was hidden by a black hoodie which hid his hands in the hoodie pouch.

"Wassup, slim?" Musa said, reaching his hand out for some dap.

Shoota removed his hand from his pocket and gave Musa some dap with a shoulder hug. Musa pulled away and stared into Shoota's eyes.

"You good?" he asked.

"Good as I'm gonna get," Shoota replied.

Musa stared at Shoota a few seconds longer before he turned around and led Shoota to the living room. Shoota stared at the back of Musa's head as he walked behind him. His heart bumped hard in his chest. His inner demons in his head were screaming

"Now! Do it now, nigga!" Shoota's hand became sweaty as it wrapped around the handle of his Glock 17 that was concealed in his hoodie pocket. Shoota attempted to pull his gun out but pushed it back into his pocket.

Musa walked in the living room and sat on the couch where he had about a half a pound of that white widow strain on the table with some backwood wraps and a .50 cal hand cannon.

When Shoota sat on the opposite side of the room from Musa he discreetly adjusted his gun to his hoodie, he had it pointing at Musa. He watched Musa's every move.

Musa could feel the tension in the room as he sat down and twisted a backwood. He wondered was the tension there because Shoota thought he was on some fuck shit or the fact he was still harboring ill feelings about him popping his B-More flunkies. Musa lit the backwood and partook in its strong effects. He inhaled deeply and closed his eyes.

That demon in Shoota's head was screaming at him, *"Pull the trigger!"*

Shoota applied some pressure on the trigger. His hand shook slightly. His heart elevated and a coat of sweat formulated in his forehead despite the house's A.C. blowing cool air.

"Pull it!" his inner voice instructed. Musa's silence was nerve wrecking "What's the business, Mu?" Shoota blurred out.

Musa slowly opened his eyes and let a cloud of smoke escape his nose. Musa's eyes were already bloodshot red and you could tell that he was already feeling the effects of the widow strain.

"New beginnings, slim! New muthafuckin' beginnings," Musa said with a smile.

Shoota didn't know how to take the comment. He removed his empty free hand and wiped sweat from his forehead. He still held the Glock pointing at Musa. He could shoot through his hoodie pocket and end Musa's life at any moment.

"How you figure new beginnings, what's new?" Shoota replied.

"Expansion, growth, money and power." Musa took another pull of the backwood.

"From where I'm sitting, Mu, you already have all those things."

"You don't and it's about time that you do." Musa made eye contact with Shoota.

Shoota didn't know where Musa was getting at with his statement. So, he stayed silent and waited for Musa to explain.

"You want to be your own boss, Shoota. I have no right to hold you back from being your own man, your own boss. I want for my brother what I want for myself. You want Baltimore and I'm gonna give it to you on a silver platter," Musa said with a smile on his face.

Shoota quickly unclutched the gun he held hidden in his pocket. His heart was really doing the running man in his chest.

"How do you feel about expanding the Money Mafia to Baltimore?" Musa asked.

Shoota's mouth was dry. All types of possibilities ran through his head. Instantly, he felt bogus as fuck knowing that he had the intention to come here and murder Musa today. Now that same person that he professed to love was offering him an olive branch and an opportunity of a lifetime. Shoota's eyes slightly started to moist over.

He quickly pulled his emotions together. "I was born to be my own boss, Mu."

"Then this the business. I'm the plug I hit you with the best Heroin the East Coast has seen since the eighties and you can take Baltimore by a storm. But you have to keep the Money Mafia's name. Can you do that?

"Money Mafia all day, every day!" Shoota replied.

"Good! This for you." Musa got up and handed Shoota a bag that held five bricks of Heroin.

Papaya every so often dropped a brick or two of dog food into the shipment on GP trying to entice Musa to explore the Heroin trade but he never did so he just kept the bricks of Heroin for rainy days. Shoota opened the bag and all he saw was him rising in the game, he already had a team set up in Baltimore. The problem was Shoota couldn't find a good enough product to invest his money in, but Musa had changed all of that. He could smell the dope's potency through the package.

"What's the bill on these?" Shoota removed one of the bricks from the bag and flipped it over in his hand.

"I got ten more of those on standby. Hit me with seventy-five a piece then when you finish the whole fifteen the price will be ninety," Musa stated.

Shoota knew that he had a deal of a lifetime, so he jumped right on it. He had enough money already to purchase the whole fifteen bricks. He knew that Musa wanted to see how fast he was going to take to move the product. He recognized a test when he saw one. If he immediately paid out of the pocket for the work that would let Musa know he didn't have a real way to move the product.

"Nigga, shake it up!" Shoota said, getting out his chair and extending his hand to Musa.

Musa rose to his feet and opened his arms wide. "Nigga, it's Money Mafia, it's all love."

Shoota stepped in and embraced Musa. "Thanks, Mu, I love you, bruh. I won't let you down, slim," Shoota said sincerely.

"Awwww, we want a hug!" Nai said, stepping in the living room with Kelly in their naked glory.

Chapter 19

Musa hated not being there to manage the incoming shipment that was coming this morning. His gut was telling him Mr. Braxton was going to be on some bullshit, so he had already laced Ace about meeting with his Parole officer and the crazy request for him to pick him up in the Porsche Taycan. Musa had a feeling that Mr. Braxton had done research on him. There was no other explanation as to how his parole officer knew about his Porsche. He wondered if it was Mr. Braxton following him when he left the barbershop.

Just in case his Parole officer was on some bullshit, he chose to ride clean and leave his gun at home. The unexpected request from his P.O. to come in face-to-face had him jittery. He turned the corner of 16th and K Street, nothing stuck out and if it did, he wouldn't have been able to tell because this downtown area wasn't a part of the city that he was familiar with. Too many law- enforcement frequent the area.

Musa pulled up in front of his parole officer's building at 10:30 a.m. sharp. He double parked next to a green Infiniti. Musa scanned the three-story tan brick building for Mr. Braxton.

"Where the fuck this clown? I'm gonna give this square ass nigga five minutes and if he don't show, I'm out this bitch. Catch me if you can. I'm the gingerbread man," Musa spoke out loud.

He sent Ace a quick text and told her he was at the P.O.'s office.

//: *Everything alright?* Ace texted back.

//: *I don't know, he ain't show yet. What's good on the demmo.* Musa typed referring to the shipment.

//: *Just pulled up, Shoota missing though.*

Musa let out an irritated sigh before he replied, //: *Handle that and I will hit you when I'm done here.*

Musa placed the phone on his lap and eyed his Rollie for the time, it was 10:33 a.m. He looked toward the entrance of his P.O.'s building and saw Mr. Braxton emerge. Musa gritted his teeth in disappointment, he was hoping Mr. Braxton wouldn't show up.

Mr. Braxton strolled to Musa's Porsche like he was the owner of the automobile and Musa was his personal driver. Mr. Braxton stood 5'11, brown-skinned with light freckles across his skin. Mr. Braxton was one of those square ass niggas who were hip with the struggle of the street life. It was evident in his body language and mannerism. Mr. Braxton's hair was cut low and wavy. He had ordinary brown eyes.

"Mr. Blackwell, my muthafucking nigga," Mr. Braxton said and push a up fist to Musa when he got in the Porsche.

Musa looked at Mr. Braxton's fist like it had dog shit on it. He reluctantly bumped fists with Mr. Braxton. Musa was confused because his P.O. had never addressed him in that way.

"This is a bad muthafucka here," Mr. Braxton said excitedly, running his fingers over the car's dashboard. "What she run you?" Mr. Braxton asked.

Musa wasn't comfortable with disclosing the price tag of the Porsche to Mr. Braxton. After all, Mr. Braxton was an acting arm of the law. Musa ignored the question and pulled the Porsche into traffic. Mr. Braxton had Musa off balance but Musa refused to let this bitch ass nigga see him uneasy.

"Where we headed? I thought you wanted to discuss removing me from parole?"

"We will discuss all of that when we get there." Mr. Braxton sunk down in the Porsche's seat with his fingers laced together resting on his lap.

Musa mugged his P.O. He wanted to slap the fuck outta Mr. Braxton. This clown didn't even know the danger he was poking at fucking with him. Musa wanted to tell him but decided to see where he was getting at with the game he was playing.

"Head over to First Street," Mr. Braxton instructed.

Musa looked at him like he was crazy, but he turned the Money Baggs up and zipped the Porsche to his P.O.'s instructed destination. The whole ten-minute drive to 1st Street Musa cut his eye over at his P.O. who bobbed his head to Money Baggs that was rapping about putting in work and selling drugs. Musa found that crazy as he turned on First street.

"Where to?"

"Down the alley behind the projects," Mr. Braxton stated as if he didn't have a care in the world.

Musa creeped down the block and made a right into the alley. Musa couldn't even come up with any reason why his P.O. would take him to his hood.

"This alley here is a death trap. A damn good place to ambush someone, stop right here," Mr. Braxton spoke calmly. He turned Money Baggs down a few notches.

Musa's heart was officially break dancing in his chest. He now knew why Mr. Braxton had summoned him. A knot formed in his throat.

"You see that dumpster right there would be the blind spot that a driver coming through this alley would never see shooters." Mr. Braxton laughed and looked over at Musa.

It was Mr. Braxton that followed him from the barbershop in the white Impala.

"What you think, Musa, is this a good alley to bring someone to an early death?"

"Mr. Braxton, I can't confirm nothing like that. I don't partake in them types of activities. I'm a legit businessman," The statement of him being a legit businessman didn't sounded convincing, and it was obvious by the dumbfounded look his P.O. held on his face.

"Pull out front we don't want twelve to stumble on us in this alley, sitting in a quarter mill' ride. They might think we're drug dealers or some shit," Mr. Braxton said letting out another laugh.

Musa pulled the Taycan around front of Ledroit Park projects. He parked on the corner. Mr. Braxton removed a black & mild from his pocket along with a phone. He sparked the black & mild without Musa to smoke in his car.

He handed Musa the phone. "Go to the photo gallery," Mr. Braxton instructed, as he blew Os in the air and watched the hustlers in front of the project run up their bag with transaction after transaction.

Musa scrolled through the pictures it was so many of them.

"I'm thorough Musa, I got it all."

Musa's hands trembled from what he saw. The pictures contained Musa making transactions, pictures of all his cribs, cars, and him wearing different drips. There was pictures of him accepting shipments from Papaya. Musa realized that none of the pictures actually had him going hand to hand. Just him putting down one bag and picking up another.

"You show me this to say what?" Musa said without a care in the world.

"I show you this to say violation of parole. You better look again at those pictures. Part of your terms of parole is you can't have contact or interact with a known convicted felon. It's clear to me that you spend too much time with David Chilson known to the world as Shoota. And there is a picture to prove that you violated parole."

"Bitch ass nigga you don't have shit. Get the fuck out my car!"

"Hold fast playboy and watch your fuckin' tone. I got more than you think. I got enough to send your black ass back to prison to be somebody's bitch. I got enough for them crackas to put a case on you. Now I can kindly go away and remove you from parole only for some petty hush money, say about two-hundred bands," Mr. Braxton said with a smile, still blowing more Os into the air.

Musa wished that he had bought his gun with him. He would have blown his P.O.'s brains all over the passenger's side of the car, and the torched the Porsche.

Musa's thoughts went to Ace and the shipment that was being delivered. He wondered was his spots being raided at this very moment. He went to grab his phone, but Mr. Braxton placed his hand over his.

"What it's gonna be, Musa? You have three more years on probation. I think two hundred thousand is reasonable to keep your freedom."

Musa felt like he had no choice, him going back would offset his business and going back behind them white folk fences wasn't an option for him. He had grinded too hard for his organization to go to shit due to him going to prison on a parole violation.

"So, you say two hundred thousand will make this situation go away and I get off parole early?"

"Soon as I get that bread I will start on the paperwork," Mr. Braxton replied.

Musa ran the situation over again in his mind. He wasn't gonna let Mr. Braxton get away with his soft press. "You have a deal, but I promise you this if you don't handle business on your end. I will have your whole fucking family murdered while you watch," Musa warned.

"Nigga, don't threaten me with a good time my word is boss now let's go get my money." Mr. Braxton stated turning the music back up.

Jibril Williams

Chapter 20

Shoota hit the ground running after Musa put them five bricks of Heroin in his possession. He put Nai in doggy style, beat her guts up for a quickie and hauled assed to Baltimore. He already had a street team on standby. He had been moving a little Heroin but he never really had enough to get a constant flow of clientele or to even consider him and his team part of the competition. Shoota's major problem though was the quality of the work he was getting when he was copping a few ounces from up NY. The work he was getting wasn't good enough to do what he'd dreamed of doing, but Musa had changed all of that for Shoota.

Shoota took the dope Musa gave him to the block of Park Heights. He sat at the table and bagged 5,000 testers. He gave out 2,000 testers throughout Baltimore. He hit East and West Baltimore passing out testers like it was candy. Four hours after giving testers out. The dope fiends came crawling in and popping up out of thin air.

"Mafia Magic!" The young boys yelled out advertising the new product.

Shoota stood across the street from the trap where his team was banging the bags of Heroin from. This was the part of the game he was in love with, that daily grind, that hand to hand hustle. To sit back and watch something he orchestrated bring in money was the all-time high to him.

"Bagz, this shit is a fucking ATM. Slim, look at these mafucka coming to cop," Shoota stated excitedly.

"I know yo', but you think we gonna have enough dope to keep 'em coming? I know you said we running this spot twenty-four non-stop." Bagz said.

Shoota hadn't conveyed to his team that he was blessed with five bricks of that raw. "Nigga, we got plenty of dope. You and Hell-Cat just make sure shit's running smooth. I want to hire more shooters. We lost Bumps and Rage."

Shoota gave the story that he caught Bumps and Rage stealing from him on some petty shit. He could not tell the truth how Bumps and Rage got bodied in his city by his best friend. If Bagz and Hell-Cat ever found out the truth they would never trust Shoota again.

"I want you and Hell-Cat to slip shifts, twelve hours a piece. I want three shooters on the block at all times. When you reup or drop money off to be put up. I want a shooter with you at all times coming and going. I don't want no lacking. We go hard like savages for the money on the grind for ninety days straight. Then we open another trap. We gonna force niggas to get with this Money Mafia movement. We give them room to work for us or buy from us. If they don't want to come on this movement then fuck 'em. Either we snatching their lives of clientele, one way or another they will bow down to the Money Mafia," Shoota said

Hell-Cat sat on the back of his white and blue dirt bike, his hand resting on the rubber grip handle of the Mack 12. His eyes stayed roaming the block. "Yo' Shoota, I'm not cut out to run a block you get better usage outta me designating your designated shooter."

Shoota knew Hell-Cat was right but he needed someone that he had a report with and could test. Besides Hell-Cat was strong, when he spoke niggas listened and got in order because they knew one thing about Hell-Cat he was about that savage life.

"I'm feeling that, Hell, but give me ninety days and we'll switch it up," Shoota reassured.

Hell-Cat nodded his head in agreement. Shoota looked down at his white gold Cellini man phase and was puzzled why his phone wasn't being blown up. He had obligations with Musa to help him secure the shipment that was scheduled to come in this morning. Shoota was so determined to get the new branch of Money Mafia rooted and grounded that he ducked out on his responsibilities of helping Musa handle the shipment. He felt kinda bad by not showing up or at least giving Musa a call, explaining why he didn't come in. He only hoped Musa could understand the need to establish his own movement. Shoota was tired and hungry but every time another thirty or forty people added to the already long line of customers. He got a sudden jolt of energy and his hunger pains vanished.

The buzzing from his pocket made him fish his phone out of his pocket. Shoota opened the text from Ace.

//: MAFIA 5! was all it read.

This was a pre-code that was established among their inner circles. This could mean only two things. Money Mafia was under indictment, or Money Mafia was going to war. Shoota hoped it was the latter.

"Fuck," he mumbled. "Aye, Bagz, hold it down. I got to handle something. Keep the shop running," Shoota said walking to his Benz truck.

***

One Hour Later

"I don't know how this nigga got all this muthafuckin' intel on me. What made this nigga focus on me!" Musa said while he paced the floor of Ace's electronic.

He balled and unballed his fists as he walked back and forth. Ace, Brim and Shoota looked on without any answers to his question.

"Maybe it's really nothing to it, Musa. I think the P.O. saw you as a quick come up. He found out who you really are, grabbed some dirt on you and used it to extort you," said Brim.

The word extort was a bad word for Brim to use. The crease in Musa's forehead deepened.

"Fuck you mean extort? Don't no nigga extort me. You said that shit to freely. What you on this nigga shaking me down?" Musa yelled.

"Mu, you tripping, slim," Shoota butted in.

"Naw nigga, I'm dead fucking serious. A nigga in my circle talking ain't no fucking way this nigga tracking me like that. To the point this nigga knows about my whole operation. I don't trust a fucking soul right now." Musa nostrils flared like a raging bull.

"So, you don't trust a nigga after all the shit we been through?" Shoota responded to the hurtful comment Musa made.

"Right now, nigga I don't even trust God. Where the fuck was you. You was supposed to be helping Ace and Brim with the shipment, but you was fucking off while this bitch ass nigga was trying to come up on me. All of sudden you M.I.A and then this shit happens."

Shoota lean back against the wall and stared at Musa like he was the dumbest nigga in the world to think he may have been on some fuck shit. They say when you getting to that money it breeds paranoia.

"Nigga, I was handling business in Baltimore establishing the new Money Mafia." When the words slipped out of Shoota's lips he regretted them.

"New Money Mafia, there's only one Money Mafia. You think you can do a better Money Mafia? Nah nigga, you should know better. Right now, we switching shit. I want all trap houses relocated. I want all routes changed. I want the whole operation stripped down and restructured. From now on everything goes through Ace. Don't come to me about no business see Ace," Musa announced.

"What about the Baltimore expansion?" Shoota asked with a little panic in his voice.

"Until I find out more about Mr. Braxton and what's his next move. That shit is dead."

Musa words angered Shoota. He stood to his feet and adjusted the watch on his wrist. He then walked up on Musa without breaking eye contact with Musa. Shoota made his mind up that he refused to continue letting Musa little boy him. He removed the Money Mafia chain from around his neck and placed it on Musa's neck.

"Money Mafia all yours, slim," Shoota mumbled, patted Musa on the shoulder and exited out the back of Ace Electronics.

Brim watched in dismay as he shook his head and departed The Hub moments behind Shoota.

Chapter 21

The look of intricacy was displayed across Ace's face. She gawked at Musa with that. *What the fuck* expression on her face. She understood the bullshit that Musa's P.O. had pulled had him discombobulated and weary, but the shit he allowed to come out of his mouth was some detrimental shit that could place him in a situation he couldn't even foresee because he had allowed his emotions to dictate his tongue. The moment Musa uttered the words that he didn't trust a soul. The vibe in the room shifted and grew darker.

Ace couldn't understand how Musa could tell his friends that he had known for years that he didn't trust them. When Musa made the statement, Ace watched the facial expression on both Brim and Shoota change. She saw that Musa's words had affected them both. She couldn't blame them, she even took offense to Musa statement.

"Musa, you know your words was fouler than a black & mild. You dead wrong," Ace said, breaking the silence.

She sat in a chair staring at Musa with her legs crossed. Musa leaned against some crates full of high-tech spyware that had become a hot item at Ace Electronics. Musa put some heat to the end of a Newport 100 hanging from his mouth.

"I'm never wrong," Musa mumbled, blowing smoke into the air.

"Nigga, you don't think telling your entire circle of Money Mafia you don't trust them, wasn't wrong? Even if you don't trust them, you don't say that shit outta your mouth unless they're staring down the barrel of ya gun and you got every intention to murder them."

"Right now, I can't afford to trust no one Ace!" Musa stated plucking ashes on the floor. "I can't trust no one in this life I'm living," Musa continued.

"Fuckk all that shit you talking, Musa. I'm not talking about some niggas you just met. I'm talking about some people that's been with this shit since day one!" Ace yelled letting her emotions get the best of her.

"When you make the type of money I'm making, the business don't allow you to trust no one. Now out the blue I got this bitch ass P.O. knowing my every move. What I'm pushing, where I'm living. What I'm selling. This nigga just pressed me for a payment. This situation is off. It's someone close to me that's behind this shit."

"Don't deflect the situation about you not trusting those close to you." Ace got out her chair and got into Musa's personal space. She had rage in her eyes. "You told a nigga that spent years in a cage for you that you don't trust him. Shoota took a gun charge for your ungrateful ass. Then you called him out on building a better Money Mafia. You knew he displayed that he wanted to become his own boss." Ace shook her head in disgust. "Then you got Brim. It seems you trusted him enough to kill One-Punch when you was facing that attempted murder charge. Do you remember that, Musa?" Tears welled in Ace's eyes. Her bottom lip trembled. "What about me. You don't trust me now?"

Musa's heart softened when Ace propose the question.

"Huh, Musa, what about me? You trusted me when I gave you them five bricks to start this Money Mafia shit. It was all trust when your ass went to jail, and I held your ass down like I was your top bitch." Tears rolled down Ace's face. "Is this why you can't love me as your woman because you don't trust me?"

The question had Musa feeling complex. He understood why Ace was bringing the past into the future. She wanted him to see that the people he said he didn't trust were the same people that had been loyal to him and that he trusted from the beginning. The question about him loving her came from elsewhere. A place he was ready to answer.

"Ace, maybe I'm wrong for saying I don't trust no one. But you can't fault me for feeling the way that I'm feeling." Musa looked down at Ace.

He plucked ashes off the Newport. He used the back of his hand to knock some of Ace's tears away. His chest hovered up and down. He could see she was upset. When his hand touched her face, she closed her eyes to savor his touch in her mind. She wanted to employ Ms. Cheryl's plans to back away from the business and see if that would bate Musa in to seeing her as more than a business part-ner, but with the current situation she understood that she needed to be by Musa's side whether he trusted her or not.

"To answer your question about why I can't embrace you as my woman—"

"Don't—don't even answer the question, Musa. Let's just fig-ure shit out with the P.O. and try to amend the tension you have unintentionally placed between Brim, Shoota, and you," Ace said, opening her eyes, stepping back out of Musa's personal space.

Musa looked at his hand lingering in the air and back at Ace face before letting it drop to his side.

"How bad you think the damage I caused is between Shoota and Brim?"

Ace let out a deep breathe. "It's bad but Shoota and Brim's love for you is strong. But you have to continue to supply Shoota for the Baltimore takeover. Don't pull the plug on him. In fact, hit him with another five bricks and tell him to go hard."

"Okay, we'll handle that and take care of Brim. What are we doing about Mr. Braxton?" Musa asked.

"I'm on it. Right now, let's put things in motion to switch the operation up," Ace stated sitting back down in her chair.

***

Brim sat in the back of The Hub of Ace's Electronic. Shoota had left twenty minutes ago. He could feel why Shoota washed his hands with the Money Mafia. What Brim had already known was coming to the light Musa didn't give a fuck about no one but himself and Ace. How the fuck could he say he didn't trust them and then turn around and instruct them to go through Ace for everything. He acted like Ace and him were the only muthafuckas who built Money Mafia.

If anything, Musa should be trusting him to run the operation. Niggas like Musa didn't amaze him though.

Musa's just like the rest of them, Brim thought.

He was just like the so-called real niggas. His day ones helped him get to the top, then they turned on them and replaced them with niggas that really don't have love for them. Brim didn't understand why the game was played the way it was by so many niggas but he refused to be one of the ones that got kicked to the curb or placed face down in a shallow grave for being too loyal. He had to change his fate. He eased the Lexus into gear and drove away with new beginnings on his mind.

Chapter 22

Six Days Later

Musa and Ace sat slumped in the back seats of the stretch Maybach. The luxurious automobile cabin was filled with exotic weed smoke. Papaya had sent the Maybach for their leisure. The Benz came with a driver. The Benz was spacious, almost living-room-like with a state-of-the-art entertainment console. The Benz cab came equipped with HD-TV and beats by Dre headphones. There was switches everywhere that put you in the mindset of an airplane. Musa tapped a floor button with his Gucci loafers and a refrigerator drawer slowly rolled open.

He removed the bottle of Don-P, ripped the foil away from the top and neck of the bottle and popped its cork, foaming bubbles erupted from the bottle opening. He quickly turned the bottle not wanting to spill the French wine on his clothes. His Adam's apple did burpees up and down in his throat as he consumed the bubbly.

Musa wasn't thrilled about celebrating his twenty seventh birthday. The encounter with his P.O. had him in a bad head space, but with Ace's persistence he submitted to a night of fun. He was having mixed emotions about what transpired between him and Shoota. He hadn't spoken with Shoota since Shoota departed from the Money Mafia. He'd given Shoota a call a few times but his calls always went to voicemail. He did get a text from Shoota first thing this morning wishing him a happy birthday. So, he was hopeful that Shoota would show up at the club to help celebrate his birthday. He didn't really want to partake in the event without Shoota.

"Nigga, treat the bottle like it's a blunt, hit it and pass it," Ace said reaching for the bottle.

Musa brought the bottle of Don-P down from his lips and let out a long ass burp. He passed Ace the bottle. She scrunched her nose and waved a manicured hand in front of her nose.

"Boi, what the fuck you been eating!" Ace said in disgust.

She traded off the burning verg Gracie for the bottle of Don-P. She smelled the rim of the bottle making sure it didn't smell nothing like what Musa had just burped up.

Musa peeped her moves. "Oh, you trying to clown a nigga. My breath always smells righteous."

"It's not your breath I smelled, it was the pit of your stomach that smelled like another person's ass," Ace mumbled taking a sip from the bottle.

"I know your ass ain't over there trying to crack jokes on a nigga with your one long toe ass."

Ace punched Musa in the ribs and frowned. She felt self-conscious, she peeked down at her foot and rolled her eyes. She tucked her foot under her. Ace was insecure about the toe on her left foot. The toe next to her big toe was super long and Ace hated it. Musa peeped her maneuver to hide her toe. He burst out laughing and choking off the exotic, tears rolled down his face. Ace sat with her lips pouted, staring out of the limo partition that separated the driver from the passengers. She took another sip of the Don-P and rolled her eyes at Musa before returning them back the partition.

Musa got his laughter under control. He needed that type of laughter in his life. The current events in his life had him so uptight.

He was now happy that Ace convinced him to come out and celebrate his birthday. He knew how sensitive Ace was about her toe. She had a mad toe issue. He leaned over and kiss Ace on the cheek. "I'm sorry, slim."

Instant contact from Musa lips involuntary made Ace close her eyes. Her love muffin between her legs became extra warm and moist and her heart fluttered faster than a humming bird's wings. A ton of emotions riffled through her. She and Musa had never really gotten a chance to have a real sit down and talk about why he couldn't see her for more than a homegirl, someone to just get money with? She wanted to take advantage of the advice Musa's mom gave her, but she couldn't even fix her mouth to tell Musa she was backing away from Money Mafia so he would make her his queen.

That shit would sound lame as fuck coming out her mouth. So, she opted to handle the situation the best way she knew how and that was head.

Ace opened her eyes and hiked her black and green Prada dress above her thighs and straddled Musa's lap. The sudden move had Musa undecided if he was gonna push Ace to the floor or not, but surprisingly he didn't. He allowed her to get comfortable. Ace locked a hand behind Musa's neck and stared in his eyes. Their gaze was intense. They tried to read each other's thoughts.

Musa hit the vega and Ace took a swig of Don-P. *Kevin Gates'* song *Jam* smoothly creeped through the speakers. Ace knew Musa could feel the heat her love muffin was discharging because she could feel his manhood stir. Ace grinded slowly on the impression of Musa's wood. His left hand gripped her hip tightly pausing her grind. The moonlight and the city streetlights provided enough illumination in the limo for Musa to see the forest green, lace panties slicing into Ace's love box. Her creases looked beautiful overlapping the crotch of her panties.

It hit Musa that after all these years of knowing Ace, this was the closest he ever came to seeing her lady garden. Her lady scent floated up his nose, his manhood twitched. He searched Ace's eyes for an answer as to why she was doing this? Their eye contact made him look away. Ace loved how it felt sitting on Musa's lap, feeling his hardness stir under her. The movement made her want him more. The sudden diverting of Musa's eyes made her panic. So, she spoke, breaking their silence.

"Why, Musa?" Out of instincts Ace kissed Musa's forehead.

"Why what, Ace?" Musa took another pull of the vega.

"Why you keep denying me, why keep denying us?" Ace kissed him again. This time she gave him a peek on each cheek, leaving behind traces of her Mac lip gloss. It was Musa's turn to close his eyes and savor the feel of Ace's lips. "Answer me, Musa," Ace whispered in his ear.

Musa opened his eyes, but he would not look at Ace. His eyes stayed on the console next to him. Even though Musa had a tight grip on Ace's waist, it only made her grind harder. At this time

Musa was brick hard and Ace was excited to know that it was because of her. She was wet, she knew she was going to soil Musa's Gucci slacks with her nectar. Thank God his slacks were black.

Ace cupped Musa's face and forced him to look at her. "Answer my question, Musa."

Musa stared at Ace for a brief moment which felt like a lifetime. Ace was beginning to think Musa was gonna reject her again.

"It's ya eyes that cause me to deny us to deny you. It's like when I look into your eyes, I'm looking into mine and every time we make that intimate connection my inner self screams, *No!*" Musa blurted out what seem like it was done in one single breath.

Ace giggled. "Mu, all this time you been pushing me away is because we both got dark grey eyes?"

"Yup!" Musa tried to turn his head from Ace but she wasn't allowing it.

She held his head in place. He didn't try to break free. The softness of her hands had Musa craving her touch.

"That's bullshit, Mu. Do you know what I think? I think you're afraid to allow someone to love you. Because you're afraid you might get hurt.

"There may be some truth to your theory, but your eyes are the biggest obstacle I have." Musa was coming clean with Ace.

He felt like a burden of two tons was lifted from his shoulders by revealing his truest reasons for rejecting Ace. Musa had been infatuated with Ace from day one. There was also part of him thinking that if he acted on what he was feeling Ace would bat his advances down because she was into women. So, he suppressed his desires, warned off by the voice in his head, telling him that Ace was off limits.

"Musa, I promise I would never hurt you," Ace said passionately.

Her lips grazed his, sending undeniable sensations to his throbbing rod. Ace grinded harder on his love muscle. She so desperately wanted Musa to park his big Mack truck in her little garage. Musa was so hard he was starting to feel some discomfort from being trap in his pants and being grinded on so viciously.

"Musa, give me a chance." Ace's lips grazed his again. Musa was hypnotized. "Whatever you lack I got you. We will balance each other out. Minor setbacks for major comebacks, a bad day I promise you a better night. All I ask that you be consistent with your love. You don't have to doubt my loyalty, you got me, and I got us." Ace riffed off her oath to Musa and ended it with her lips making full contact on his.

Their tongues touched and twirled upon contact. Musa hungrily sucked on Ace's tongue. He palmed Ace's backside like two basketballs and pulled her closer to him. Ace cuffed his face in her hands and fed Musa her hot wet tongue.

Something felt different tonight from the kiss they shared at Ace's crib. There was the feeling of no hesitation, no restriction. Ace was convinced that Musa, her true love, would till her garden and plant his seed in her soil. The limo cruised into the parking lot of the Stadium Strip Club. Ace was in the process of removing her dress. Musa stopped her by grabbing her hands. He kissed her again before he pulled back and visually took her in. His inner self screamed no but his heart and the thumping pulse between his legs told him to throw caution to the wind and love Ace like he always desired.

"Hold up, slow down." Immediately Ace knew Musa was on some bullshit. She snatched her hands out of his. "Hold up, baby you're gonna get the D tonight that's fo sho. I just don't want your first time to be in the back seat of a limo."

"This is not just a limo, this is a muthafuckin 'Maybach!" Ace said cutting Musa off.

Musa chuckled. "You're right but I want shit to be right so let's go in here, turn the fuck up for my birthday and the afterparty will be tonight at my crib just me and you in our birthday suits. Let's make this shit official, Ace. I'm tired of playing games."

Ace smiled the smile of an angel. "You promise?" Ace asked.

"On everything I love," Musa confirmed.

"Well, let's go show these bammas how Money Mafia's King and Queen show out," Ace said dismounting Musa's lap right before their driver opened their door.

Jibril Williams

Chapter 23

The whole Money Mafia family were waiting at the Stadium entrance for Musa and Ace. They refused to enter the club without them. Musa stepped out of the stretch Maybach, dressed in a Gucci shirt with the green and red stripe going across the middle, rested nicely over his all-black Gucci slacks. His size twelves were crisped, creme colored Gucci loafers with the green and red band going across the top, he looked paid. The saucer sized double M chain he had around his neck made him look like he was ready for a rap video.

Ace strutted next to Musa in her pair of forest green Louis Vuitton red bottoms. The body clinching Prada dress that covered her curvy body was glove fitting tight. You could see her every curve. The way she wore her mohawk with the green ends had made her look straight stunna sexy. Ace dripped with drip, her double M chain and her Audemars Piguet made her look like she was worth a million bucks.

When Money Mafia saw their leaders they gave a round of applause.

"The thoroughest nigga in the city has finally grace us with his presence," Brim said with a bright smile on his face as he embraced Musa in a bear hug.

Over the years, Brim had proven himself to be very loyal to Musa and Money Mafia. Musa had established a lot of love for Brim. When Musa approached the statement, he made the other night about him not trusting a soul. Brim let the statement roll off his back like a duck let water roll off his. He assured Musa that he knew he was under a lot of stress. Musa dapped it up with the rest of the team. Jus-Blaze, Sharkhead and Stink. The only person that was missing was Shoota and that kinda saddened Musa, but he didn't let that be known. He was there to celebrate his 27th birthday, nothing more nothing less.

When Money Mafia entered the Stadium the club's occupants was getting it in. Musa knew the owner Kirk was getting that bag. The scene made Musa want to get his feet in the night life. There were strippers there that Musa had never seen before. Musa's entourage had all eyes on them. Every stripper they walked past licked their lips seductively and bared dollar signs in their eyes. A few niggas from Oxon Hill, Maryland that Musa declined to do business with was there clownin' the fuck out. They were about twenty deep, throwing blueish bills in the air over a group of strippers.

Musa nodded in acknowledgement but he could see salt in the eyes of Pop-Roc. He was calling shots for Oxon Hill Mafia Boyz. Musa made a mental note to make plans to push into Pop-Roc's territory. Musa smiled at Pop-Roc and patted the humongous Money Mafia chain that hung around his neck. The chain alone let Pop-Roc know he wasn't eating nowhere on Musa's level and the tightness in Pop-Roc's face let Musa know that.

The walk to V.I.P was like a red-carpet event. Muthafuckas was gawking and light weights snapped pictures. There was a few strippers giving lap dances who'd stopped serving their clients just to get a good look at Money Mafia. The Stadium Strip Club was one of Washington D.C.'s hot spots. The club brought in some of the best and baddest bitches the country had to offer. They catered to celebrities, athletes, dope boys and men and women of power.

The Money Mafia hit V.I.P and immediately ordered thirty bottles of Moet and two gallons of Patron. A train of twenty strippers entered V.I.P. Musa and his team selected fifteen of those strippers and dismissed the remaining five due to them not being being thick like the Money Mafia liked their women. Ace had put all this in order. She had been planning this event for weeks. She knew ninety percent of the women that came through the Stadium because Jassii was her girl and worked there.

The V.I.P room brought back memories of her lover. There would be times she would miss and crave Jassii. Ace would come to the club in the middle of Jassii's shifts. She would order two bottles of some bubbly and hit V.I.P for a private lap dance with Jassii, Stadium's top dancer. Jassii's private show would quickly turn into her eating her box out in V.I.P.

Musa sat on a small couch with four beautiful women seductively dancing in front of him. Ace looked on in lust but with a slight tab of jealousy tugging at her heart. She had claimed Musa as hers. She couldn't wait until she got Musa to his crib so he could claim her body. He already had her heart. It had been years since Ace had a real man inside of her.

Her stomach fluttered thinking about how Musa would feel tapping her inner walls. But she would deal with that at the end of the night. She walked over and reached in the Louis Vuitton bag Musa brought in the club with him. Ace grabbed a stack of money, joined Musa on the couch and begun feeding bills to the women dancing in front of them, they made her mouth water.

***

What do you say, Mr. Shoota?" The beautiful Mexican woman asked, sitting close to him in the corner of the Stadium.

Shoota was a little uncomfortable with how close the woman was sitting to him. Her soft whisper in his ears and the sweet smell of Gucci For Women made it hard for him to concentrate. There was a pinging in his head that the woman sitting next to him was a Fed. The woman sitting next to him was named Emma Coronel Guzman, she was offering him a plug that would link him to the Sinaloa Cartel. Shoota sat there calmly weighing out how he would reply to the beautiful woman and her proposition.

He watched Musa and Money Mafia enter the club like they owned the whole fucking club and the city which in reality they did own the city. There were no one in the city doing it like the Mafia. Shoota observed the hate Pop-Roc held in his eyes as Musa walked by. He was aware of Musa rejecting the idea of Money Mafia doing business with Oxon Hill Mafia Boyz.

Ace had hit him up and pleaded with him to come celebrate Musa's birthday. He started to decline but thought against it. Musa was still his friend despite that they couldn't be on equal terms in the same business they'd both helped build. Shoota wasn't a hater especially when it came to Musa, so he agreed to come out, and plus he already had pre-shopped for Musa's birthday gift. It was only right that he bought it out and gave it to him.

Ace also told him she had something for him from Musa. He already knew what that meant. So, he came with the money he owed Musa for the five bricks of dope. He had the intention to pop a bottle or two with Musa for old time's sake, hit Musa with his bread, grab the work that Ace got for him then bounce to Baltimore and get back to the money.

"Sorry, I don't think you and me are in the same line of business. I don't sell drugs, I'm an entrepreneur," Shoota said, throwing back a shot of Henny.

A flash of ignorance flashed in the eyes of Emma. "Mr. Shoota, I don't like to be played with. I know who you are. It's obvious you don't know who I am." Emma crossed her legs causing her Chanel dress to raise farther up her thighs. Shoota peep her brown-skin and licks his lips.

"Once again, my name is Emma Coronel Guzman. I'm the wife of a very powerful man. My husband is El Chapo." Emma reached over into her Chanel bag and removed her phone.

She showed Shoota pictures of her and El-Chapo on vacation in foreign lands, sitting by Olympic sized pools, soaking sun rays. Shoota had seen El-Chapo's face many times before on the news, so he knew the woman was stating facts and she wasn't bullshitting on who she was. So, he wondered was her business legit. The notion ran through that he could possibly be sitting next to the plug of a lifetime. He went all the way in boss mode. Now he definitely knew he wasn't sitting in the presence of a Fed, but a potential means for him to build his own empire. He didn't want to rush into nothing after he still had all the intentions to cop his work from Musa.

"Okay, you El Chapo's wife. Now what?" Shoota said nonchalantly.

"Well, let's do business, papi," The way papi rolled off Emma's tongue sounded sexy. "I'm going to be honest, Shoota. My plan tonight was to come here and give your partner Musa an offer to switch plugs from Papaya the Los Cinco Diablos to the Sinaloa but I saw you here and decided to make the underdog the top dog. I like the energy that pumps from you."

Shoota was blown by how much Emma knew about the Los Cinco Diablos plug and Papaya. She must've been about her business. She'd done her homework, but there was one problem, he was no longer a standing member of Money Mafia and from Emma's statement about making the underdog the top dog. Shoota knew he was no longer a member of Money Mafia. Shoota wanted to cease the opportunity for himself and be his own boss.

"Listen, Lady Emma, I'm not partners with Musa anymore and I think you know that. But we are still tied by the heart and bond. I have to have my own team that I'm building. I need a solid connect. I would like to do business with you. I'm gonna be honest, Musa is loyal to Papaya he would never cut ties with Papaya."

Emma stared at Shoota's lips and eyes trying to detect some deceit. Satisfied there was none. She reached back in her Chanel bag and removed a square gold foil. She scooted closer to Shoota. She pushed the package down the front of Shoota's pants. She grabbed a handful of his manhood and made eye contact with him.

"Mr. Shoota that is the purest Heroin that Sinaloa has to offer. Push it out to your people, get back with me and we will discuss prices and quantity."

Shoota's manhood grew in Emma's hand. "I like you, Shoota." Emma gave it a tight squeeze. "If things go well maybe you can see what I feel like and F.Y.I, I've never been with a black man." Emma removed her hand and passed Shoota her card with her contact information on it. "You have one week to get with me about business. After that my number will change and I will approach Musa." A barmaid came and placed two bottles of Moet on the table. Emma stood to her feet. "The champagne is on me, papi. Treat Musa to a bottle and tell him it's from the queen of the Sinaloa Cartel."

Shoota watched Emma Coronel Guzman's back side sway back and forth. For the first time Shoota noticed that Emma wasn't alone two Mexican females getting lap dances not too far from them got up and exited the club with Emma.

Jibril Williams

Chapter 24

Shoota walked in the V.I.P section where the Money Mafia was getting it in and the strippers were getting their money's worth. They were sweating out their lace fronts, but it was worth it. The floor was covered with bills. A dancer by the name of MiMi Suno from New York was spread wide on her stomach doing the cry baby dance. Every time she'd bring her hips up off the floor and slammed them down, her ass trembled and shook like an earthquake and more bills would pollute the air and trickled down on top of her.

Starr X and Christina Foxx were going toe-to-toe with a nasty twerk off. When the two would make it clap their pussies winked and blew kisses at Money Mafia men. The action caused the hustlers to toss more money in the air. Shoota stood in the entry way of V.I.P with two bottles of Moet in his hand.

These niggas really clowning in this bitch, Shoota thought.

He watched Ace enjoy a lap dance from Vanity Momentum, Jassii's best friend. He watched Ace's fingers disappear in and out of Vanity's opening. He shook his head and smirked. He guessed Ace was over Jassii sucking that dick with the quickness.

He could tell that Musa was drunk and overwhelmed with excitement. He stood over top of three women who were engaged in a high-performance threesome. *Pay Ash Cash* screamed out in pleasure from Chyna Soul's tongue rapidly beating on her clit.

Musa yelled, "Money Mafia all day every day!"

Nia the G.O.A.T fingered Chyna Soul from the back while she twirled her own fingers on her pearl tongue. Musa must have felt Shoota's eyes on him because he diverted his eyes from the threesome taking place at his feet and focused them. A broad smile appeared on his face. He threw his arms in the air with a fist full of bills in each hand.

"My muthafuckin' nigga!" Musa yelled.

Shoota smiled back and threw his arm in the air. He was still holding the bottles of Moet in his hands.

Musa trucked through the crowd stepping over strippers and U.S currency like it was toilet paper. He embraced Shoota in a bear hug. Shoota could tell that he was good and fucked up because he lifted him in the air like he was some high school chick and every nigga knew nothing was gangsta about being lifted off your feet.

"Hold up, nigga! Put me down, nigga!" Shoota said playfully but was very serious.

Musa complied, "My big head ass nigga. You know a party ain't a party without you," Musa slurred.

Shoota wanted to run the situation with Emma by Musa. He just wanted Musa's opinion from his perspective, but he could tell Musa wasn't in any shape to talk business or discuss the encounter with Emma. So, Shoota told himself he would put that on the back burner until another day.

"Slim, you know I wouldn't miss this shit for nothing in the world," Shoota stated.

Musa seemed to sober up a little. He grabbed Shoota by the shoulders.

"I'm sorry, Shoota, my bad. My nigga, sorry for all the dumb shit I been doing," Musa said sincerely.

Shoota still wanted to address their issue, but that would wait until Musa was in a better state of mind.

"I hear you, Musa. We will talk about our past and our future. But not tonight, it's about you tonight so let's turn up, bruh," Shoota stated and handed Musa a bottle of Moet.

They both pop the corks on the bottles and turn them up to their lips before announcing Money Mafia. Shoota fished the box out of his pocket and handed it to Musa. Musa opened it and examined the custom-made platinum Yacht Master. The face on the watch was big. The biggest Musa had ever seen. The Bezel in the watch was dipped with green diamonds. Musa removed the Audemars Piguet that he had on and replaced it with the Yacht Master.

Instantly, Musa fell in love with the watch. "Thanks, Shoota."

"It's nothing but love. It's nothing but Money Mafia all day every day," Shoota spoke over the loud music.

Ace walked up and hugged Shoota. "Thanks for coming."

"No problem, I got that gwap for Musa in my truck."

"Alright, we'll get to that but let's celebrate," Ace said waving a few girls over who didn't hesitate to get it popping. Even though the club was love it was evident that real scene was V.I.P with Money Mafia.

Pop-Roc and his team watched strippers after strippers headed over to V.I.P. Money Mafia was rotating strippers like a nigga rotates drawers. The women that work the club who didn't have the privilege to work V.I.P was fine, but they were nothing like the women that was up there with Money Mafia. Pop-Roc wanted to see Mimi Sumo. That was one of the reasons why he came out tonight.

He was in his feelings when the club owner Kirk told him that Mimi Sumo was unavailable tonight, she was booked for Money Mafia's personal entertainment for the night. Being the businessman Kirk was, he offered to send Mimi Sumo protege Storm. Pop-Roc felt offended that he was offered something less than what he wanted. He felt like he was a man of high regards, and he should get what he wanted.

Pop-Roc even requested for Jassii's presence but he was told that she wasn't working tonight. The strippers, the Oxon Hill Mafia Boyz had was tiring. Pop-Roc wanted some of the action that was transpiring in V.I.P.

"Come on, we hitting V.I.P!" Pop-Roc announced leading the way to V.I.P.

The group of women scooped their earnings off the floor and went on to the next customers. When Pop-Roc made it to V.I.P. He was stopped by a big ass bouncer with acne scars on his face and rocking a mohawk.

"Aye, slim, this is a private affair!" The bouncer announced before Pop-Roc and his entourage could fully make it to the completely.

"Man, we ain't trying to hear that sucka shit. We up in this bitch. Oxon Hill Mafia Boyz in the building!" Pop-Roc stated with a little heat in his voice.

The Patron Pop-Roc was drinking, had him feeling untouchable. The bouncer placed a hand on Pop-Roc chest, which he knocked away with aggression.

Brim saw the commotion and jumped to his feet throwing a stripper to the floor who was consumed with gyrating her lady parts on his lap. Stink and Jus-Blaze followed suit. Ace tapped Shoota and Musa, getting their attention. The bouncer radioed in for assistance.

"A nigga trying to die tonight!" Shoota said, walking up in Pop-Roc's face.

Pop-Roc stood about three inches taller than Shoota but he was a skinny nigga way out of his weight class to fuck with Shoota. But the nigga Pop-Roc was like a pit bull. He had no fear in him all he had in his heart was win, lose or draw.

Musa pushed his way through the crowd. The group of strippers scooped money off the floor and huddled in the back of V.I.P hoping shit didn't pop off between the two groups.

"No one has to die tonight, but that's your call to make. We just came to party. We come bearing bottles. Why not two teams come together that's getting gwap out here in these streets. Why can't we turn up together and pop a few bottles and share some pussy together?" Pop-Roc stated looking over Musa and Shoota's shoulder and making eye contact with Mimi Sumo.

Who rolled her eyes in dismay at Pop-Roc for interrupting her cash flow. She thought Pop-Roc was lame as fuck for that.

"You all got V.I.P rocking harder than a muthafucka," Pop-Roc stated focusing his eye back on Shoota and Musa.

Musa stepped a little closer to Pop-Roc. "This my birthday and this is a private party. This Money Mafia, we buy and pop our own bottles among Money Mafia. We don't do handouts. Matter of fact go back to your little spot on the floor. Money Mafia will send you a few bottles on us," Musa said with his lip curled up.

The alcohol Musa had consumed had him ready to go to war. The tension rose quickly from those small exchange of words. Nine bouncers and the club owner Kirk came pushing through the crowd getting between Musa and Pop-Roc.

140

Money Mafia

"You know, Musa, you're getting kinda big headed with this Money Mafia shit. You not the only one eating out here. Any of you damn sure not the only ones with an army that's willing to die for you on your command. You need to start recognizing that every king falls."

"Nigga, fuck you!" Musa yelled trying to push past the bouncers to get to Pop-Roc.

Ace grabbed the back of Musa's shirt trying to hold him back. The bouncers separated the groups and Kirk was able to calm the situation with providing a few free bottles to both sides to kill that shit and see each other in the streets and not in his club.

Musa gave the nod, and everyone went back to partying. He partied harder, he wanted Pop-Roc and the suckas to know that they didn't faze him or his team. Musa waved Brim over.

"Wassup, Boss!" he replied a little tipsy.

"Tomorrow give them Oxon Hill niggas a hundred rounds from that Draco, Money Mafia style," Musa whispered in Brim's ear.

"Say less, slim, I'm on it," Brim retorted.

Jibril Williams

Chapter 25

"Aye, slim, it was fun but a nigga gots to run," Shoota said, dapping it up with Musa.

"Come on, Shoota, I know you not letting Pop-Roc run you off?"

"Musa, you should know better than that," Shoota replied.

Musa smiled. "Bruh, I wasn't trying to play on your ego." Musa embraced Shoota in a bear hug. "Thanks for the watch, nigga. I know you spent the whole safe on that," Musa whispered in Shoota's ear as he embraced him.

"Nah, it wasn't the whole safe, but you could get it if you need it."

"I'm good, slim, my money stay long," Musa bragged.

"Speaking of long money, I got some to add to that," Shoota said, breaking Musa's embrace.

"Good! Give that to Ace when she hits you with them other joints. I can see the B-More move being a very big come up for you," Musa stated seriously.

"I intended it to be," Shoota said with a chillness in his voice.

There was a quietness between them for a few seconds and for the first time Musa felt Shoota was walking away from Money Mafia forever, but he didn't know how to address the awkwardness between them.

"You know, Mu. If you need assistance with them Oxon Hill niggas, don't hesitate. I'm still Double M all day every day, just in another city."

Musa smiled and dapped Shoota up. He flagged Ace over and told her Shoota was leaving. He took a seat on the V.I.P couch and watched Ace and Shoota leave out of V.I.P

***

"I can't believe this bitch is being flakey ass fuck tonight," Jassii said to herself as she sent her best friend Vanity Momentum a text.

Vanity texted her and told her that Shoota was at the club, hugged up with some Mexican bitch. Then she was in V.I.P acting a damn fool, throwing money over naked hoes and partying with the ops. Jassii knew about Musa's birthday, that was all Ace could talk about when she was planning the event. She'd asked if Shoota was attending Musa's birthday party, but obviously he had a change of heart because she got word that he graced Musa's party with his presence. He was still there because his truck was sitting on the other side of the parking lot next to a stretch Maybach.

Every time Jassii texted or called Vanity and didn't get a reply, her blood boiled. She felt like everyone had played her. Vanity was supposed to be loyal to her, but she was up in the club shaking her ass in a nigga's face for dollars when she needed her to be her eyes and tell her what Shoota was doing in the club. She had fallen in love with Shoota. Now she was sitting in the parking lot of a strip club wondering who her man was throwing money on.

It really bothered her because she was the top bitch in Stadium but yet, her nigga was disrespecting her with the same bitches that looked up to her when she walked through the doors of the Stadium. It was clear why Shoota kept prolonging robbing and helping her kill Ace for fucking her brother Jacob over. Shoota still had love for Ace.

Jassii couldn't take it anymore. She checked her phone one last time. She was gonna go inside the club to see for herself how Shoota was really rocking out of her presence. There was no text from Vanity. Jassii sent her a quick text telling her best friend she was a piece of shit. Jassii got out of her car and popped her trunk, she kept a slew of wigs of different colors. She wanted to be low-key when she walked in the club. She rambled through the trunk for the perfect wig.

***

"Here is the bread for Musa," Shoota said, handing Ace a small Louie V duffle bag.

144

She exchanged it for the bag she was carrying. She had the bricks stashed in the trunk of the Maybach. Ace looked around Shoota's Benz truck, she felt like she had been inside the truck before, even though she knew she'd never taken a ride with Shoota before.

"Thanks for coming out tonight, Shoota. I know that our boi Musa has been testing our loyalty, but he means good, Shoota. He really does," Ace said sincerely.

Shoota had just closed the hidden compartment for the bricks.

"I know he means well, Ace, but I have to move on and become my own—"

Boom!

The loud bang on the window made Shoota and Ace jump. "Bitch ass nigga that's how you doing it!" Jassii yelled as she bounced up and down on her toes.

When she closed the trunk of her car, she saw Shoota was in his truck and from the silhouette inside the truck she could see he was with a woman. Without thinking she ran up to the truck to bust Shoota's ass.

"Who the fuck is that?" Ace said trying to see what bitch was going ham on Shoota.

Seeing Jassii on the driver's side demanding Shoota to open the door. Instantly, she felt anger. Her mind went back to the video of Jassii sucking someone's dick in a Benz. She knew it was a Benz because of the Mercedes Benz emboss on the steering wheel. Ace eyes shot to Shoota's steering wheel and the Benz emboss stared back at her. She hauled off and greeted Shoota's chin with her fists.

"Bitch ass nigga you fucked her! It was you in the video?" Ace's fists weld down on Shoota.

He tried to get away from her little bee stingers. To elude Ace's punches Shoota exited the truck only to be faced with Jassii swinging wildly at him.

"I can't believe you out here fucking with the ops. I shoulda never trusted your ass." Jassii swung on Shoota.

Shoota wasn't with getting a beat down from no broads. He grabbed Jassii by the waist and spun her around pinning her in a bear hug.

By this time Ace made it out of the truck and was around the driver's side, she took the opportunity with Shoota holding Jassii back from attack. She snatched Jassii's wig off her head and punch her right in her muthafuckin' eye.

"Agggh, Bitch!" Jassii screamed, grabbing her eye and kicking at Ace. "Shoota, let me go!" Jassii demanded.

Shoota's mind was getting the ten bricks out of D.C before the police showed up. He let Jassii loose, she and Ace locked eyes like two fighting dogs.

Jassii clawed at Ace's face while Ace threw lefts and rights catching Jassii with all types of combos.

"Bitch-I-gave-your-ass the world!" Ace stated every word and every punch.

Somehow Jassii got her hands around Ace's neck, flung her to the ground and out of nowhere, Jassii produce a knife. She brought the knife up in the air, the knife blade gleamed in the moonlight. She brought the knife down forcefully with intention of bringing serious body harm to Ace, but her arm was stopped in mid-air.

"Bitch, what the fuck you think you're doing?" Shoota stated angrily.

He twisted Jassii's wrist, and the knife fell free from her hands. He snatched Jassii back. Ace jumped to her feet.

"Aye, Ace, I'm sorry for this bullshit. But we gotta deal with this shit another time. We got a bag of money and a trunk full of dope. We need to get the fuck from this spot."

The club's door opened, and the Stadium bouncer came pouring out the club. Someone must have told them that there was a fight in the parking lot. Ace looked like a mad woman, her hair was fuck up and her Prada dress was ripped. Even though she wasn't ready to let the matter go, she knew Shoota had a point. The respect she had for Shoota died right there in that parking lot. So, she walked around, got the bag of money out of Shoota's trunk and placed it in the trunk of the Maybach.

146

Jassii was still trying to get away from Shoota to get at Ace. Her eyes were puffy. Ace walked around to where Shoota stood. She had tears in her eyes.

"I hope them ten bricks take you where you're trying to go in this game because you will never eat off Money Mafia's plate again." Ace wiped her tears away from her face.

Her words were offensive to Shoota and he let his emotion get the best of him just as always.

"Bitch, I'm gonna eat regardless. Fuck you and Money Mafia!" Shoota didn't mean the words that came out of his mouth, but Ace's statement ignited something in him.

"And bitch you, when I'm riding Musa's dick tonight, I will be forgetting that you ever existed. Fuck you, I hope you die, Jassii!" Ace said walking away.

"Fuck you to, Ace. I hope you die too, bitch."

"Bitch shut the fuck up and get in the fucking truck," Shoota ordered.

Jassii she complied.

Shoota had his mind on getting far away from the Stadium.

Jibril Williams

Chapter 26

Ace came back in the club headed straight for V.I.P, she could not wait to tell Musa the grimy snake shit Shoota was doing behind her back with Jassii. She had her mind set that she'd never fuck with Shoota again. If Musa still rocked with him or did business with Shoota, she was willing to walk away from him and Money Mafia forever. Ace was so mad she wanted to kill. She had that killer activated in her since she'd killed her stepbrother. She had a taste for blood.

Ace had a tightness in her chest, she needed to release her anger. She guessed someone informed Musa that some shit jumped off with her in the parking lot. Because he was coming out of V.I.P looking crazy with the whole Money Mafia behind him. Pop-Roc and his team was still clowning. When Ace tried to walk past them one of Pop-Roc's men grabbed her ass. The dude that handled Ace, palmed her ass so viciously. The unexpected touch brought Ace off her feet, reflexes guided her to spend around on her heels and punch a brown-skinned dude in his mouth.

After that everything seem to move in slow motion. The punch popped dude's head back a little. It was obvious that he wasn't expecting to get his lips pop for his actions, so he returned Ace's punch with a backhand. Money Mafia bared down on dude like a bad storm, bottles started flying and punches followed. Pop-Roc popped off on Musa, Musa bumped right back with a right hook putting Pop-Roc on his True Religion back pockets. Musa didn't even celebrate his victory over Pop-Roc. He went straight to work trying to bring hell to the Oxon Hill Mafia.

Jus-Blaze was getting tapped danced on by a group of Oxon Hill Mafia niggas. Musa scooped up two Moet bottles littered across the floor. He brought one to one Jus-Blaze's assaulter's head, blood gushed between his fingers. Brim was duking it out with two niggas at the same time. He was doing good holding his own, but Oxon Hill Mafia was too damn deep they outnumbered Money Mafia. It seemed like the club split in half, half was team Mafia, and the other was team Oxon Hill Mafia everyone was fighting, strippers and all.

The bouncers rushed back in from outside and started spraying muthafuckas with pepper spray. The pepper spray made it hard to breath, bitches were choking and fighting with their eyes closed.

Ace had a broken bottle in her hand, she was giving a nigga the sharp end of it. Musa grabbed her.

"Ace, lets bounce, slim." Brim was already helping Jus-Blaze off the floor.

Everyone was making their way out the door, trying to get air in their lungs to help kill the burning sensation the pepper spray caused.

The Money Mafia made it out of the club without further incident. The parking lot was crowded and muthafuckas scrambled to their cars before the gunshot rang out and the police got there. Brim helped Jus-Blaze in his whip and Stink faded into the crowd after he watched Musa and Ace hop into the stretch Maybach and pull off.

Ace immediately got a bottle of water out of the fridge and soak a hand towel. She wiped Musa's face and arms. She wanted to wipe anywhere his skin may have been exposed to the pepper spray. She then got a fresh towel and bottle of water and repeated the process on herself. The cold towel felt good on her skin.

"You good, Ace?" Musa said hitting everyone on his phone making sure everyone was alright.

"I'm good, but I'm trying to ride tonight though. Let's swing past the crib and change clothes. Then we can slide through Oxon Hill and show them niggas what that hundred round do," Ace said.

"Shit, I'm down with that—" red and blue cherries lit the back of the limo up, halting Musa's statement. "Damn!" Musa mumbled.

"We good just sit tight, Musa. We clean," Ace assured.

The limo pulled over and a police car pulled up behind them with its high beams on. The police car lights had the inside of the limo bright. Two officers emerged from the car. One stood at the back of the Maybach. A tall white officer approached the driver's side and questioned the driver about where they were coming from. Musa and Ace couldn't hear much of the officer's questioning, but they did make out the words strip club and the altercation. The officer retrieved the I.D. He then came back, knocked on the window and motioned for Musa to lower his window. Musa did.

"It's a good night for the strip club, ain't it?" The tall white officer smiled.

The question was more of a question to catch Musa in a lie. If he said no, the officer would have made it known that the driver already told him they were at the strip club.

"Every night is a good night for a strip club," Musa said with a smile.

The officer didn't like Musa's smart-ass response. "Do you know anything about the altercation that took place at the Stadium strip club?"

"I didn't see an altercation. I did hear something happened tonight, but I didn't see anything though, officer."

"What about you, Miss lady?" The officer asked, bending down and looking at Ace who sat next to Musa.

"I didn't see anything either," Ace replied.

The officer paused and looked back and forth between Ace and Musa. Before he asked for identification, Ace and Musa handed the officer their respectable I.D.s. He went to run their names through their system.

Musa and Ace sat in the back of the limo in silence. "You know what, Ace? We done had one crazy ass night. Let's just deal with them Oxon Hill niggas another day. We can just shower at your place and cross into unknown territory."

Musa reached over and wrapped his hand around Ace's. Musa's warm touch made her stomach flutter, and the folds of her love box became moist. Finally, Musa was going to claim her body and become her king. She had desired this for years and finally it was going to happen. The officer returned to the car. Things seem different. His partner already had his hand drawn as he approached on Ace's side of the limo.

"Mr. Blackwell, please step out the car and keep your hands where I can see them," the officer was stern, and his voice was laced with seriousness. He had his hand on the butt of his Glock while it rested in its holster.

"What's going on, officer?" Musa asked

"Step the fuck outta the car?" the officer yelled

Musa looked at Ace, panic was in her eyes. Musa reluctantly stepped out of the car, the cop forced him on the trunk of the limo and placed a pair of handcuffs on him.

"Officer what did I do?" Musa asked

"You have a warrant for your arrest."

"For what?" Musa asked in confusion

The officer smiled. "For parole violation."

***

"Bitch, I can't believe you showed your stupid ass up to the club acting like the silly ass hoe you is!" Shoota yelled at Jassii who was balled up in the passenger seat of his Benz truck. Shoota had been back handing her every few blocks.

"Why you had to go a fuck with her, Shoota?" Jassii asked.

"I don't fuck with Ace. I went to grab some work from her!" Shoota yelled, reaching over and punching Jassii in the face.

I thought you was gonna help me get back at Ace for doing that foul shit to my brother.

"Bitch, fuck your brother. He deserves everything that happened to him. That nigga was fronted some work and his bitch ass ran the fuck off with the work. He's lucky Ace didn't kill his ass," Shoota said.

Jassii's phone vibrated, it was Vanity texting her. Then her phone vibrated with an incoming call from Vanity. Jassii ignored the call.

"Shit, for real, you should be the one that got bodied. If I didn't have some type of feelings for you, I would kill you for doing the shit you did tonight," those words made Jassii look at Shoota.

This was the first time Shoota had ever expressed some feelings toward her. Shoota brought the truck to a stop at the light before he hit B.W.I Parkway heading to Baltimore.

"I only act like this because I love you, Shoota."

A motorcycle pulled up next to Shoota's Benz.

"I wish you could see my true love for you and look past me just being a stripper. I'm a whole woman, Shoota. I have a lot to offer."

Shoota listened to Jassii, he did feel her words. He knew Jassii was a real go-getter and he need someone like her on his team.

"Listen Jassi—"

Boom! Boom! Boom! Boom!

Bullets ripped through the driver's side door and drilled into Shoota's body. Jassii screamed and got low, but it didn't stop her from catching a bullet to her head. The driver of the motorcycle popped off more shots from his Mack-12 and more shots hit Shoota. The light turned green and the motorcycle sped through the light.

Shoota's truck coasted to the middle of the intersection, blood rushed from the fresh bullet hole. He could hear his heart thump in his chest. He touched his neck, he could feel blood rushing from it. His hands trembled and he choked on his own blood. The truck cabin started to spinning and he felt light headed. It burned his chest when he tried to breath. All of sudden he felt cold. He fought to keep his eyes open, it was impossible, so he let the darkness take him over.

Jibril Williams

Chapter 27

Thirty Days Later

Ace sat in her rental Ford Focus sitting in front of Mr. Braxton house that he shared with his wife and sixteen-year-old daughter. She blew P.C.P smoke out the window as she checked the silencer to the end of her Glock 40. She'd been watching Mr. Braxton ever since he blackmailed Musa for the two hundred and fifty bands. When Musa called and explained the situation. She placed a tracking device in the bag of money, which led Ace to Mr. Braxton's crib in Temple Hill Maryland. Mr. Braxton put shit in the game after he snatched that money from Musa.

The slick ass nigga placed a warrant for Musa's arrest the same day Musa gave him that money. He had no intention of letting Musa off parole early. It was all game. Musa was immediately sent back to prison and the parole board wanted him to serve the remainder of his parole time in prison which was 2 ½ years. Mr. Braxton had shattered Ace's world. She never thought she would have to live life without Musa again.

Mr. Braxton didn't know the type of pain he had caused her and with a she-devil lurking at his doorstep, he was about to find out. Jassii wanted to know why Mr. Braxton did what he did. What was his motivation? She opened the Ford's door and her Timberland work boots hit the ground. She slightly closed the door not wanting to bring attention to her. The P.C.P had her numb to the world, it motivated her to detach from reality and turn off all human emotion for life. All that motivated her to seek revenge for Musa and herself.

Ace walked light as a cat burglar up the walkway to Mr. Braxton's home. On her way she passed by two brand-new Monte Carlos, one white and the other grey. The paper tags on both cars alerted Ace that they were new and probably purchased with the money Mr. Braxton burned Musa for.

Ace walked on the porch and before she knocked on the door, she peeked through the living window catching Mr. Braxton's eight-month pregnant wife Gina between her husband's legs giving him oral pleasure. Their sixteen-year-old daughter couldn't have been home, there would be no way her parents would perform such activities in the living room if their daughter was in the house. Well, that's how Ace rationalized it in her mind. Ace surveyed the street before she knocked on the door.

Ace quickly glanced at her watch, it read 9:15 p.m. She could hear some movement on the other side of the door before the porch light came on. Ace tilted her head down a little.

"Who is it?" an angelic voice came through the door.

"Ummm, yes, I think I saw someone trying to break into your car," Ace said, putting on her innocent performance.

Without another word being exchanged Gina started unbolting the locks on the door. All Gina could think about was someone stealing her new car that her husband bought her. She threw caution to the wind and snatched the front door open. When she stared in the eyes of Ace and peered at the gun she pointed directly at her stomach, threatening the life of her unborn child, she knew that she had been bamboozled.

"Bitch, step back into the house and kill the porch light."

Gina became scared but obeyed her intruder. Her hand quickly killed the porch light, and she took steps back allowing Ace into her home. Ace kicked the door closed with her foot.

"We have money—"

Ace held a finger to her lips silencing Gina. "Living room," was the only command she gave Gina.

Gina slowly walked into the living room. During the brief walk Ace examined Gina. The woman was light-weight and beautiful. The sweatpants she wore fit her nicely, showing off the curves of her pregnant body.

"Who was it, baby?" Mr. Braxton asked when Gina walked back into the living room.

He looked confused when he saw Ace standing behind his wife, but he knew what it was about when he saw the gun in her hand. He recognized Ace from dropping off the money that he blackmailed Musa for. His only concern was how she found him. He was very cautious not to bring trouble to his doorstep. When Ace dropped the money off to him and Musa. He had Musa drop him off at Union Station then he caught a bus to New York, spent a week there, rented a car and drove home. None of his personal information was listed.

"You came for the money?" Mr. Braxton asked.

"Ronald, what's going on?" Gina asked crying.

Gina was really confused now. She wanted to know what was going on and why this woman was in her house with a gun.

"Nah, I'm not here for the money. I'm here for some answers. You earned that money, it's yours. But just so you know, I'm dead ass serious about these questions I'm about to ask."

Phat!

The gun in Ace's hand sparked and a bullet blew out a chunk of meat from Mr. Braxton's thigh.

"Aggghhh—shit!" Mr. Braxton hollered.

Ace removed a pair of zip ties from her back pocket, secured Gina hands behind her back and laid her down on the floor. She then went and sat on the small table in front of the sofa. Mr. Braxton's grey sweatpants were covered in blood. He held his hand over the bullet hole in his right leg trying his best to suppress the bleeding. Ace sat there and watched him for a full two minutes. Pain and panic was written all over his face. The P.C.P Ace smoked had her feeling weird, almost devil-like and wanting to do something forbidden.

"Now, Mr. Braxton, you know a bitch ain't playing. I will bust another hole in your ass. So, answer my questions truthfully."

Mr. Braxton nodded in agreement.

"How did you get on to Musa and the Money Mafia?" Ace sat in front of Mr. Braxton with her legs open like a dude, her gun dangling in her hand between her legs.

Mr. Braxton looked like he wanted to hesitate, but he was motivated when Ace pointed her gun at his other thigh.

"Brim put me on to Musa and the Money Mafia. I'm gonna need a doctor soon."

"What the fuck you say?" Ace said, jumping up to her feet. She couldn't believe the name Mr. Braxton had just dropped.

"It—it was Brimain. This was all his idea?"

"Mr. Braxton, get to talking before I kill your bitch ass!" Ace hollered.

"Brim is my nephew. I hadn't met him until a few years ago. I ran into his mother at my brother's One-Punch's funeral."

"Stop! One-Punch is your brother?"

"One-Punch is my youngest brother!" Mr. Braxton said through pain.

Ace was mind blown about these facts. She wondered if Mr. Braxton knew Brim had killed One-Punch. His own father.

"Keep going," Ace demanded.

"I saw Brim's mother Helene at the funeral. She told me that One-Punch had a son named Brimain. I wanted to meet my brother's only seed. I wanted to help Brim get out of the streets. That was my good deed for One-Punch. I wanted to save his son because I failed to save him. I allowed the streets and drugs to take over my brother's life.

"Me and Brim hit it off decently. I expressed to him one time how I wanted to get the muthafucka who killed my brother. Some years later, Brim came to my house and told me that Musa had my brother killed because he was a witness in a case against him. I did some investigating and found out One-Punch was testifying against Musa for shooting him. Come to find out Musa was already on my caseload. I was his parole officer. Brim came and asked me to violate Musa's parole and have him locked up." Mr. Braxton was really spilling the beans now, he kept talking.

"Brim told me he worked his way under Musa. He wanted to take revenge on him for ordering his father's death. He gave me all the info on Musa so I could blackmail him. He gave me pictures and addresses."

"What is Brim's plans now that Musa is locked up?"

"He's gonna take over Money Mafia and kill Musa when he comes home. He wanted Musa's plug. The only way he can take over Money Mafia he has to have the plug."

Ace's mind was racing. She was scheduled to meet the plug soon. If Brim was planning to secure the plug that meant he was going to try to kill her. Ace's heart started beating harder with anger.

The thought of Brim betraying Money Mafia and Musa. Everything Mr. Braxton said made sense. She had to warn Musa about Brim…

"Please don't kill us!" Mr. Braxton said. "This was all Brimain's idea, not mine or my wife's," Mr. Braxton pleaded and started crying like a baby.

His questions and pleas snapped Ace away from her thoughts. She looked at him with an irreligious smile. She up the Glock and popped five muffled shots into his face causing the back of his head to explode and soil the sofa cushions with his blood and pieces of his brains.

Gina wept on the floor uncontrollably after watching her husband's executions. Ace studied her handiwork and the craving of doing something Satan-like was still upon her heart like a bad heartbreak. She stood up and walked over to a crying Gina. Ace stared down at her with no sympathy in her eyes. Gina was so shaken up over witnessing her husband's death that she couldn't even plead for her or her unborn child. Ace looked down at the lady's huge stomach and the craziest idea came to her mind.

She located the kitchen and removed a knife from the knife holder that were stationed on the kitchen counter. She also grabbed two dish towels off the handle of the oven. When she got back to the living room, Gina was trying her best to get to her feet, but having her hand tied behind her back and being eight months pregnant it was an impossible task.

Ace walked over to Gina. "Bitch open your mouth," she demanded pointing the gun at Gina's head. Gina complied and Ace stuffed both dish towels in Gina's mouth. More tears spilled out Gina's eyes, Ace didn't care. She took the knife and cut Gina's shirt off her, exposing her pregnant belly. Ace yanked Gina's sweatpants around her ankles and didn't hesitate. She swiftly and like an expert surgeon dragged the blade of the knife under Gina's stomach.

Gina let out a roaring scream, but it was muffled by the towels. Ace sliced deeper with a second slash, blood and a gush of water spilled out of the bottom of Gina's stomach. Gina felt like she was gonna die.

Ace had no regards for Gina. She stuck her hand inside of Gina's stomach. Gina could feel Ace's every touch. "I'm gonna give you a chance to meet your baby before you die. Now that can't happen if you faint on me. If you do that, you're gonna miss it," Ace said as her hand moved around inside Gina's stomach.

Her hands touch a pair of small feet. She grabbed them and pulled them, a wet, sticky sound could be heard. When Gina's infant was pulled from her stomach. Soon as air hit the baby lungs it cried and lit the house up.

"It's a girl," Ace said, cutting the umbilical cord separating the baby from mother.

She laid the baby on Gina's chest. Gina was fading in and out. She lifted the gun and sent three shots to Gina's stomach. The P.C.P had Ace in another world emotionally. She grabbed the towels out Gina's mouth and wiped her hands removing Gina's blood. She tucked her gun and fished her phone out of her pocket. She dialed Ms. Cheryl number. Ace walked through the three-bedroom house, checking to make sure she wasn't leaving anything of importance. Even though she didn't travel down into the bedrooms.

Mrs. Cheryl picked up on the fourth ring. "Hello."

"Ma, this is Ace. I need you to do something important. When Musa calls tell him to call me immediately."

"Okay, but what's going on? I can hear it in your voice," Ms. Cheryl had concern in her voice.

Ace didn't want to alarm Musa's mom, but shit was real. She stood at the front door with her hand on the knob. "Just tell him don't trust Brim," Ace said as she opened the door to leave behind a bloody crime scene.

When she opened the door, she was face with Brim and he had a gun pointed at her chest.

Boom! Boom!

His gun shots lit up the night.

Chapter 28

Three Days Later

As soon as Musa heard the guard's keys unlock his cell door, he opened his eyes and planted his feet on the cold concrete floor. Being back in the confines of Wackin Hunt prison made Musa feel trapped and enslaved. He took in his current living condition, two grey lockers bolted to the wall, a stainless-steel sink and a toilet. This was definitely a downgrade from the baby mansion he resided in only thirty something days ago. Being back in prison wasn't sitting well with him. He badly wanted answers to why Mr. Braxton had violated him after he gave him the money to not violate his parole?

When Musa learned that he'd be doing the remainder of his time he had left on parole behind prison walls it was a crushing blow to him. 2 ½ years was a long bid when you had unattended millions out there. Ms. Cheryl had most of the money stashed and placed in stocks and bonds. Something that Papaya had schooled him on many years ago doing his first bid. Musa rubbed his hand over his waves. He needed a haircut, bad. He told himself that he would hit the barbershop today after he tried to get a hold of Shoota and Ace.

He'd been trying to get a hold of Shoota since the first day he got arrested but had no luck. He was thinking Shoota was still harboring ill feelings toward him for stating that he didn't trust a soul. A flash of anger hit Musa, because the thought of Shoota running off with the ten bricks he fronted made him want to lash out at something. It seemed Ace had disappeared on him also. Ace was supposed to look into Mr. Braxton for him. They were in constant contact with each other until a few days ago.

Ace was supposed to meet the plug, but she couldn't be reached, so he and Papaya agreed that Brim would handle shit and keep shit rolling until Musa gained his freedom. Brim could pull this off if he listened, paid attention and moved with caution. He would have to bring stink and Jus-Blaze all the way in the loop. Even though Musa allowed Brim to take rein of Money Mafia, he still felt uneasy about the decision. The good thing about being back at Wackin Hunt prison was that Papaya was there and he had access to almost everything. Musa expressed to him a few days ago that he needed a phone. Papaya offered Musa access to his but Musa declined.

He was still a boss, and he wanted his own shit. Papaya wasn't happy about seeing Musa back in prison. Musa explained the events to him of his P.O. and how the bitch ass nigga shook him down for two hundred and fifty bands and still flipped him and violated his parole. Musa asked Papaya to have his people look into Mr. Braxton. Musa wanted to find out who he was. Who his family was. He wanted to know his children's names. He even wanted to know the names of his pets if he had any. Papaya told him he would get on it asap for him.

Musa got up, took a piss, washed his hands and took care of his hygiene. Musa had only been back in Wackin Hunt prison for a week, after spending almost three weeks in D.C. jail. Musa's locker didn't reflect that he'd just got there over a week ago. He already had several pairs of brand-new shoes under his bunk and his lockers were stacked to the T. He was riding solo in the cell so he was happy about not having to share the cell with someone and he could use the single cell time to focus his thoughts.

A knock came to Musa's door. Musa spun around to see a Mexican dude standing at his door with his face covered in tatts. Musa did not know the dude and could read death in his eyes, but Musa still waved the guy in his cell.

"Wassup?" Musa asked as soon as the dude stepped foot in his cell.

"Me name Chino, Papaya send this for you." The young Mexican dug in his dip, removed a galaxy 21 and handed it to Musa.

Musa flipped the phone over in his hand and smiled. "Alright thanks, Chino."

"I need to know what brick you want to loosen up so you can hide the phone behind it?"

Musa showed Chino the small brick under the lockers and Chino marked it with a brown mark. "I will be done by lunch," Chino stated and left the cell.

Musa put the phone under his pillow and walked out of his cell with his cup. He went to the hot water dispenser and got a cup of hot water. He didn't need the hot water, he just wanted to check the unit out to see who was watching and what was going on before he jumped on the phone. In prison you never knew who was peeping your moves.

Musa walked back in the cell and threw the flap up in the cell window. He powered up the phone, he was happy to see that it had a full life on the battery. The first person he tried to call was Shoota. The phone informed him that the phone was now not in service. Frustration came upon Musa instantly. He tried Ace's phone and he learned that her message box was full and couldn't leave any more messages.

Musa began to worry about Ace. He immediately called Brim who picked up the phone on the third ring.

"Who this?" Brim answered.

"Musa, nigga! How shit go yesterday with the demonstration?" Musa asked, talking in codes about the shipment.

"Hold up, slim, how you calling me?"

"You know I'ma boss, so a nigga made boss moves. This my line you can hit me on in case of an emergency," Musa whispered not forgetting how thin the walls of prison wall could be at times.

"Okay, bossman, I hear ya. But shit went smooth. I met the handler so we good, two hundred nothing less."

"Alright that's what's up stick to the strip and bring Jus-Blaze and Stink all the way into the loop. We need them niggas to step it up."

"I think we still should set out to take over Capitol Heights," Brim replied

"Nah, don't fuck with that right now. What you do is get them niggas buying from us. The Mafia has become unstable. Shoota missing and Ace is missing have you heard from either?" Musa asked.

There was a pause on the phone.

"Nah, slim, I ain't heard from them I guess they're doing them?" Brim replied

"You say that to say what?"

"Bruh, I don't mean shit by that. All I'm saying is we got to keep the Mafia up and running and they're off somewhere and can't be found. I think they somewhere together." Brim was trying to cloud Musa's mind with bullshit.

Musa didn't even feed into it. He knew better of Ace. "Just keep trying to get a hold of them." Musa didn't even tell Brim that Shoota's phone was disconnected, or Ace voicemail was full.

"Aye, I got you, bossman! One," Brim said and hung up.

Musa took in the way Brim said bossman, it was lace with sarcasm. Musa was stressed the fuck out. He knew calling his mom would bring him a sense of peace. She always knew how to calm that storm within him. He dialed his mother number and even though it was early in the morning she answered the phone like she'd been waiting on him.

"Hello!"

"Hey, Ma!"

"Musa, that you?" Ms. Cheryl said alarmed.

"Yeah, Ma, what's wrong?" Musa asked.

"Can we talk on this phone?" Cheryl was from the old school she knew better than to speak something on a hot line.

"This my phone. Yeah, you can talk. What's up?"

"Shoota and Ace, baby! It's all bad, baby, it's all bad! The police came to my house about him. He had my address on his truck's paperwork. They found his truck shot up on B.W.I Parkway with Ace's girlfriend Jassii dead in the truck she was shot in the head. They believe Shoota was shot and kidnapped. They haven't found his body yet."

Musa's heart sunk to the pit of his stomach. He wondered why Shoota was with Jassii? "Ma, when did this happen?"

"On your birthday, baby."

This meant the situation happened after Shoota left the party.

"What's going on with Ace?" Cheryl bust out crying. "Ma, what happened! What's going on," Musa started to panic.

"Ace is in the hospital. She was shot two times in the chest.

"What!" Musa yelled, raising his voice forgetting he was in a prison cell.

"That's not the worst part of it, Musa. It's all over the news. She killed your parole officer and tried to kill his wife and child. She was shot by someone leaving the crime scene. They don't even know who shot her, Musa." Ms. Cheryl started to cry again.

Musa's mind was racing as he tried to process the info his mother had just given him. He needed to get off the phone and think shit through. "Ma, I'm gonna call you later," Musa said

"No, hold up, there's something else. Ace called me and told me to have you call her asap and not to trust that boy Brim. She told me that and I heard gunshots. I think she was talking to me when she got shot."

Now Musa's head was really spinning. "Okay, Ma, has anybody come and talked to you about this?"

"No!"

"Well, if they do, tell them you don't know nothing and the last time you talk to Ace she called and said that she loves you. And hung up," Musa informed, he knew he was going to get some blow back from this. He just wanted his mom to be prepared.

"Okay, son, I love you! Be safe in there," Ms. Cheryl said disconnecting the call.

Musa did the same. He powered off his phone, stashed the phone in the bottom of a cracker box and placed it in the back of his locker after then stacked food products in front of it. Musa wanted to walk the track and sort the situation out while the prison inmates ate breakfast in the chow hall. While he was walking out of the cell two Mexicans were there to remove the brick from under the locker so he could have a place to stash his phone.

Jibril Williams

Chapter 29

Brim blew purp in the air and silently praised himself. He orchestrated a helluva plan to become Money Mafia's top boss. Everything fell in his favor. Shoota left Money Mafia, Ace is fighting for her life and if she does survive from the gunshots. She would spend the rest of her life in prison. She wasn't stupid enough to go to trial after what she did to his uncle and wife. The state of Maryland would surely put her ass on death row for what she did. It was sheer luck that Brim was able to catch Ace coming out of his uncle's house. He had gone to the house to give his uncle Rob some money for coming through and playing his role in sending Musa back to prison.

When he walked up on the porch, he heard his uncle scream. When he looked in the window, he saw Ace standing over his uncle with a gun and Gina lying on the floor. He had intention to rush in to save his uncle but when his uncle started spilling his guts about how they met and that One-Punch was his father. He was like fuck it. He was gonna body the whole fucking house. He could not let Ace leave with the information that his uncle gave her. He watched Ace kill his uncle and gut his uncle's wife Gina. He waited on the porch for Ace to come out and it was like deja vu all over again when he stood on a porch and waited for his own father to walk out a house so he could kill him. When Ace walked out of his uncle's house, he put two slugs in her chest and disappeared like a thief in the night.

The only thing Brim had a problem with was that he still had to go through Musa to get the product. Musa was playing middle-man between him and the plug. If he had direct access to the plug Brim would have been murdered Musa. So, he had to lightweight play by Musa rules. If he could connect with a plug that could supply grade A work like Musa was getting, he would abandon ship and leave Musa in jail to deal with the reality that he'd been beat and Money Mafia had a new boss.

***

Ace laid in bed staring at the hospital's white walls, the TV was on mute as the news reporter spoke and told the world about her dirty deeds of killing Mr. Braxton and cutting his wife's baby out her stomach. The whole world viewed her as a monster. People were making comments like, *Whoever shot Ace should have killed her. That's what a person deserves. Who opens a woman's stomach and removes her baby then shoots her?* The Washington hospital center staff even treated Ace differently.

Gina survived her attack. Reports reported that Gina was blessed, and it was a miracle she and her baby survived. Ace knew she was in a fucked- up situation. Her tight shackle to the rail of her hospital bed confirmed that.

She didn't give a fuck, though. She would not beg for her freedom or beg for the cracker to spare her life. Her mind was on Brim and his betrayal. It was killing her inside and adding pain to the pain she was experiencing from her gunshot wound in her chest. She needed to get word to Musa about Brim. It would be impossible due to her circumstance and being isolated from everyone else. Her mind shifted to Musa.

She closed her eyes and thought about him and the texture of his skin. The softness of his lips. The way he threw his head back when he laughed. She thought of her king. Her savior. The man that loved her for no other reason but to just love her. Musa was her everything he meant to her what no other man ever meant to her. Musa gave her a home at Money Mafia.

Brim and Shoota thought she was second in command of Money Mafia because of her ties to Musa as a friend but it wasn't. It was because of her sacrifice she had made for Money Mafia. Ace's mind dipped deeper to relive something she had suppressed deeply so long ago.

She knocked on Musa's bedroom door after Ms. Cheryl had let her in the apartment that they had on W street.

Musa yelled, "Come in!" When he made contact with Ace's grey eyes he rushed to her. "What's wrong?" he asked

"He did it again," Ace said, falling on Musa's bed crying. "I swear I'm gonna kill his ass this time. I'm not gonna keep letting him violate me, Musa," Ace cried balling her fists up. She could still feel her step-brother's semen seep from her womb into the lining of her panties. She felt sicken feeling Pumma's man fluids crawling inside her.

"Where that nigga at now, Ace?" Musa asked lifting the edge of his mattress and removing a pearl handle .25 Cal. The gun looked small in his hand. Musa went to grab his leather jacket off the chair.

"No, I'm gonna do it, Musa. I have to do it. I need to do it. If I let you do it. I will always feel like a victim," Ace announced and jumped up from the bed blocking Musa's path.

She looked him in the eyes and knew without a doubt Musa would kill for her, but she needed to know that she could and would kill for herself. Musa's chest rose and fell with anger at the thought of Pumma forcing his way on Ace.

Ace felt something that could not be explained at the time knowing that Musa would step out on a limb and murder in her name. Ace loved Musa even more for that. He always showed her that he was her protector.

"Show me how again," Ace requested leading Musa to the mirror that was stationed over the brown wooden dresser.

Musa put the gun in Ace's hands and stood behind her. He wraps his hand in hers and helped her point the gun at the mirror. "All you have to do is point and squeeze the trigger. There will be a loud pop that will frighten you. But long as you're behind the gun and pulling the trigger the pop won't hurt you," Musa coached Ace.

Musa's chest was on Ace's back. Ace felt safe there with Musa. She stared back at Musa through the mirror's reflection. She could see herself pulling the small gun trigger over and over.

"I can do this, Musa. I'm ready to do it. I already set everything up like we planned."

"Are you sure, Ace? Murder is something serious."

"And so is rape, Musa," Ace retorted.

Musa could feel the dedication in Ace's voice, he knew she had her mind made up. All he could do was ride out with her. "Let's go then."

The whole ride over to Pumma's apartment on 14th and R Street NW the car ride was silent. The possibilities played out in each of their minds. Musa wasn't okay with Ace facing her abuser alone, but the determination in Ace's eyes told him that she was capable of handling her business.

Ace's palms were sweaty and her breathing was shallow from fear. However, she didn't want to accomplish nothing else at the moment but to air Pumma's creep ass the fuck out. Pumma was her step-brother he really wasn't even that. He was his mother's boyfriend's son. Pumma thought he could distinguish the fire she had in her for the same sex. Pumma thought in his sick mind that if he forced fed her some dick, she would overcome the desire for women.

Ace had told her mother a few times about the assaults but her cries went on deaf ears. Her mother faulted her for what was happening to her and didn't want to make an issue of it in fear that she would lose her boyfriend over the matter. Ace even put it out there that this would be the second man she lost because she was dealing with sexuality issues. Ace was crushed by her mother's words. So, she began plotting the death of Pumma with Musa. She had played and replayed her plan over and over in her mind.

When Ace and Musa reached R Street. The night sky opened up and it begin to rain. Musa pulled his Chrysler in the alley behind Pumma's building, put the car in park and faced Ace.

"Listen, Ace, you don't have to do this. I can do this shit for you," Musa said.

Ace contemplated Musa's assistance, but the rage in her core wouldn't allow her to accept his help.

"Keep the car running," Ace whispered as she exited the car and made her way between Pumma's apartment building.

She walked between the gateway. The sky lit up with lightning and rain beat down on her skin. The cold rain soaked her shirt. The coldness hardened her nipples.

"A perfect night to serve a dish of revenge," Ace mumble.

Money Mafia

She pushed two milk crates under Pumma's bathroom window, stacked them on top of each other and stood on them to put her eye level to the window. She patted her back pocket and felt the weight of the six shot .25 Cal. She pushed the window up and lifted herself up into the window. The window was located over top of the bathtub. Ace's wet Air Maxes hit the bathtub without a sound. She could hear music being played somewhere in the apartment. She was grateful for that, she grabbed a towel off the towel rack and wipe her prints of the window and windowsill.

She and Musa had been planning this for a long time. Earlier when Ace was asked to stop by Pumma's apartment to grab some money for her mom, Pumma took the opportunity to violate Ace sexually. She could still feel Pumma's presence between her legs. After the rape, Pumma let Ace use his bathroom to clean herself up. Ace washed between her legs while tears roll down her face. When she was finished, she was sure she would kill Pumma tonight. She unlocked the bathroom window and headed straight to Musa's mom's apartment.

Ace walked out of the bathroom with the small gun in her hands. The music was coming from the living room. Ace had been to Pumma's apartment many times. It was a two-bedroom one bath and small kitchen. She knew no one was in the master bedroom because it sat directly across from the bathroom. She had a full view of the empty bedroom. Ace tiptoed toward the living room. She passed the second bedroom, it was empty too. When Ace walked in the living room, Pumma was sitting on the sofa with his back to her.

"Aye, slim, I got the work. Fall through and make sure you bring that gwap!" Pumma said and hung up his phone then set it next to him.

The image that played on the 42-inch Samsung TV had Ace ready to spill her stomach on Pumma's floor. Two butt ass naked men were on the screen, in the 69-position slurping each other's penises up and down. Ace became really angry. The nigga Pumma violated her because she was gay but the whole time he was a homo thug on the low. Ace walked up behind Pumma and place the gun *to the back of his head. Now standing over Pumma Ace could see that he was naked waist down and he was slowly stroking himself.*

When the cold steel touched Pumma's head, he froze. He heard the hammer on the gun cock back. "I don't want to die. The work is on the table in the bag."

"You raped me because I was gay, but you a downlow, homo thug?" Ace said with a voice full of tears and anger.

Pumma heard Ace's voice and kinda relaxed a little. "Ace what the fuck you doing?" Pumma was relieved that it wasn't some niggas there to jack him for the bricks.

"I'm here to murder your ass," Ace cried out.

Pumma's body stiffen he could sense the seriousness in Ace's voice. Ace wanted to pull the trigger but something in her wouldn't allow her to. She took a deep breath. Pumma could sense Ace hesitation. He was starting to think he could maybe talk his way out of his current situation, but then he heard a male's voice.

"I'm here with you Ace."

Ace felt a pair of arms wrap around her waist and she knew it was Musa. Ace still had the tip of her gun rested on Pumma's head.

He put his mouth next to Ace's ear. "This nigga who rape you, Ace. Show no mercy, pull the trigga, Ace," Musa spoke with firmness. Ace still hesitated. "If you don't pull the trigga, he's gonna forever violate you," Musa coached.

Visions of Pumma pumping in and out of her soiled her thoughts. His natural scent violated her nose. The thought of him on top of her made her skin damp.

"Squeeze, baby girl, blow this nigga's shit loose," Musa whispered in Ace's ear.

A calmness came over Ace and she pulled the trigger.

Pow!

The small gun clapped in her hand and a small hole was instantly drilled in the top of Pumma's head. The bullet exited through the bridge of Pumma's nose.

Ace stood there and took in Pumma's slain body, she felt nothing.

"Let's go, Ace," Musa spoke calmly in Ace's ear.

172

She turned around and faced Musa. "Thank you, Mu."

"Come on, Ace, we don't have time for this let get the fuck outta here," Musa complained.

Ace nodded. "Hold up!" Ace said, walking around to the front of the sofa. She grabbed the black bag, brought it back to Musa and opened it, five bricks stared back at them. "You can have them, but I want to be all the way down with the team. You, Brim and Shoota."

Musa saw the five bricks and the doors the drugs was getting ready to open for them.

"Ace, I swear you'll eat at the table right next to me off the same plate," Musa said with so much sincerity that Ace couldn't do nothing but believe him. "Now let's go, Ace."

"One more thing," Ace said, grabbing Musa by the shirt.

"What!" Musa said getting upset with Ace.

"This right here stays right here ya. Can't tell no one, Musa. Not Shoota or Brim."

Musa looked at Ace and understood the importance of keeping her secrets a secret. "Ace, with these bricks we about to see a new life and this dead ass nigga will go to my grave with me. I will go the distance to protect you."

Ace opened her eyes and wiped away her tears. She had to get word to Musa soon as possible. She had to warn her love.

***

Musa sat on a bench on the rec yard and watched the inmates walk the track in circles like they were everyday cattle. The niggas on the basketball court hooped and talked shit. There were people playing poker for money. Others slapped a blue hand ball against the wall like they didn't have a care in the world. It was a whole fucking world going on outside of the prison walls. How could these muthatfuckas just live like it's important? They are incarcerated. It was weeks ago that he was on the other side of those walls living life.

Now he was just a fucking prison number. He reflected on what his mother told him about Ace and Shoota. He couldn't believe

Shoota let some nigga catch him slipping. Musa's eyes misted thinking about the outcome of Shoota's life, knowing Shoota he wasn't gonna give up the cash or no info. Then Ace's beautiful face flashed across his mind.

"Damn, baby girl, why couldn't you leave that shit alone?" Musa spoke to himself. He knew if it was the other way around, he would have done the same for her.

"Morning, Musa!" Papaya said, walking up and taking a seat next to him on the bench.

His two bodyguards posted at opposite sides of the bench. Their dark ray beams made it difficult for you to see their eyes. Musa looked at Papaya awkwardly about his good morning greeting. Nothing was good about this morning or any other morning that he would be waking up behind prison walls.

"Wassup, Papaya!" Musa uttered.

Papaya could feel Musa's foul energy and Papaya knew it was only due to Musa coming back to prison and leaving his empire at the hands of another.

"You know, Musa, sometimes when they take you out of the game it doesn't mean you are not part of the game. Even though you not on the floor with the ball or out in the field running the ball you're still in the game—" Papaya paused as two Aryan brothers jogged past them on the track, then he continued, "You're still in the game because you're the coach," what Papaya was saying made complete sense to him. "The coach is the biggest part of the game. You will never see a team without a coach, Musa. Money Mafia is your team and you're the coach. And to be honest in this game it's best to coach and be outta sight than to coach and be on the side lines. The coach that plays the side lines makes it easy for the Feds to put a case on him."

Musa's brain was like a sponge, soaking it all in. He understood everything Papaya was dropping on him. The game didn't stop, you have to learn to play the game from both perspectives. From a player's aspect and a coaches one. The time he will be away from the street will allow his name to cool off and with Brim out there handling Money Mafia business. In everyone's eyes he would be the new boss and everyone's focus point. Musa felt uneasy about that part, but he could only hope that Brim acted according and how he told him to.

"Now, Musa, I have something I need you to see. Before you react you're gonna have to make a coach decision. You asked me to look into that P.O. Mr. Braxton and I did." Papaya pulled out two pieces of paper. "The first sheet is all the info on Mr. Braxton all the way down to who his children are. The second page is of his brother and his brother's children."

Musa read the papers and when his eye read the name, Terrance Braxton. Musa stopped reading and pondered the name until it shine bright like a prism in his mind. He recognized the name, Terrance Braxton was One-Punch's government name. He had learned of it when One-Punch was gonna testify against him for shooting him. When Musa read who One-Punch's only child was, he surely thought he was gonna die, his heart thumped hard in his chest. Brimain Braxton was One-Punch's son, Musa had Brim kill his own father.

Musa had handed Money Mafia over to Brim. Musa looked from the papers into the eyes of Papaya, then back to the paper to read them. Ace must have discovered that Brim was his P.O.'s nephew and that One-Punch was his P.O.'s brother. That's why she sent word through his mom not to trust Brim. Musa had his thinking cap all the way on and his unanswered questions coming together like a fat girl's butt cheeks. His mom told him that Ace was shot on the phone with her. Ace was found shot coming out of his P.O.'s house. They never identified her shooter so he would bet his life that it was Brim who shot her.

Musa always had the feeling that it was someone was close to him who fed Mr. Braxton info on him and Money Mafia. Now he knew who it was and he knew why. He looked back at Papaya and quoted something that Papaya once conveyed to him.

"Life's greatest dangers often come not from external enemies, but from our supposed colleagues, friends, and family who pretend to work for the common cause while scheming to sabotage us," Musa recited without a stutter.

Papaya smiled and applauded Musa. "I see you have been pay-ing attention. It's always the ones close to us that's easy to deceive us," Papaya stated stroking his thick mustache.

Musa looked into his mentor's eyes, and something was slightly off with him. Papaya's body language was on point, but his eyes searched Musa for something. Papaya's last statement replayed in his head and he wondered if Papaya said too much when he stated, *"It's always the ones close to us that easy to deceive us."*

"So, what's the play coach?" Papaya asked, testing him.

Musa looked away from Papaya and focused on the group doing pull ups on the pull up bar. He then looked back at Papaya. "I keep feeding Brim the work, let him run the bag up. Let him continue to build Money Mafia. I sit here and coach from behind the scenes. Let him think he's running shit. Once I'm free I smash his bitch ass for his betrayal."

Papaya smiled for the second time. "Now you're thinking like a real boss. You keep that shit up, you'll control your own cartel in no time," Papaya said jokingly.

Little did he know he'd just planted a seed in Musa's head.

Chapter 30

"Money Mafia's new fucking king!" Brim screamed at the top of his lungs.

He stood on top of a table in Dream's strip club. He pitched bundles of five-dollar bills in the air. The strippers around his table were going nuts, they were butter bald naked making it do what it do. Club Dream was letting Brim have his way in the club. He stood on the table shirtless, showing off his abs with a cold Money Mafia chain swinging from his neck. He tossed handfuls of bills in the air. The bluest green bill looked funny on the strip club light. Brim loved to floss and flex. The last four months had been a blur. The money was coming so fast he couldn't even count it.

He strategically took over seventy-five percent of Capitol Heights Maryland traps, pushing out Money Mafia's product and he had moved in with such quickness in District Heights the niggas out there just fell in line like ducks. Brim had called a truce with Pop-Roc and linked up with the Oxon Hill Mafia on some business shit, the money did a double up. Brim was moving double the shipment Musa was moving when he was home and he did this all in four months. He and Pop-Roc were making so much money together he was thinking about bringing Pop-Roc in, giving him a seat at the table and merging in both Mafia families.

He just had to figure out how to tell Musa. Musa still hadn't introduced him to the plug yet. It didn't sit well with Brim that Musa hadn't made the connection with him and the plug. Brim knew Musa was stalling. Brim wasn't no fool, he knew if Musa controlled the plug then he would still control Money Mafia even from behind bars. That made Brim still a worker for Musa. This knowledge led him to seek out his own plug but the product coming across his table was trash.

He was determined to find a plug even if he had to fly down to Mexico and introduce himself to one of the cartels. He took that play out of American Gangster's playbook. He just hoped the cartel would let him leave with his life if he couldn't secure a deal with them. Until then he was gonna keep getting this money and let Musa continue to think he was the mastermind behind Money Mafia.

Brim had heard about Shoota's truck being shot up and Jassii being found dead in his truck. For the life of him, he couldn't wrap his mind around what the fuck happened to Shoota. The word on the streets was that some niggas snatched and murked him. Shoota's body was never recovered.

Brim was still waiting to hear some feedback about his uncle violating him and him shooting Ace but Musa never mentioned a word to him. So, that left Brim with the conclusion to believe Ace was having difficulties getting word to Musa that he had shot her since she was sitting in a Maryland jail and Musa was doing a violation bid in Wackin Hunt prison.

Pop-Roc jumped up on the table with Brim and added bills to the forecast of money raining down on the strippers.

"Damn, Brim, you see that bitch!" Pop-Roc yelled, tossing money over a stripper with butterfly wings tatted on each butt cheek.

Every time she bounced and clapped her ass to the beat her butterfly wings would flap.

"Yeah, we taking shawty and a group of her friends to the W tonight. I got the camera crew meeting us there," Brim said over the loud music.

Brim and Pop-Roc had put some money together and invested in a small porn business called Butt Busters Adult Entertainment. The amateur porn was becoming a hot commodity on Pornstar. To keep Butt Buster content fresh Brim or Pop-Roc would entice strippers from different clubs to join them at a location and have them bust it open on camera for a few dollars and they were doing these two to three times a week and going live on Youtube.

"Ah, shit you just made the night. It's going to be a long one." Pop-Roc smiled.

***

Ace walked down the tier, her eyes stay alerted as she moved slowly. The two holes she had in her chest were healing good but still had her moving awkwardly after four months. The other women housed in her unit gave her space but she often caught dirty looks from them. They'd been seeing and reading in the newspaper about what she'd done. She gained no stripes from them for hurting a pregnant woman. So, she kept to herself. Ace walked into her cell with her shower bag in her left hand.

"You good, Ace?" Tammy asked as she looked up from a fashion mag she was flipping through.

Tammy was a short, brown-skinned chick with light green eyes and a mean temper. A lot of women stayed away from Tammy, she was known to throw punches first and ask for names later.

"Aye, girl, I'm good. I just can't wait to get back to a hundred percent so I can start addressing some of these stares."

"What you got beef? Who is it?" Tammy jumped off her bunk and slid her feet in a pair of Reebok Classics.

Tammy was what kept Ace living in peace in the unit. Tammy didn't judge Ace for her crime, she knew she didn't know Ace's struggle, so she could never judge her. Tammy was one of those people who didn't have a lot and by her not having the basic things in life made her bitter which resulted in her fighting when she was confronted with a uncomfortable situation.

"Naw it's no one in particular, just muthafuckas in my face like a washcloth," Ace said, stepping in a clean pair of panties and pulling a white cotton sports bra over her head and securing her breasts.

"Okay, let me know, girl. Cause I'll ride for you," Tammy stated sincerely.

Ace knew her cell mate's words had truth to them. She wasn't sure if it was because she had Ms. Cheryl drop a few hundred on her account when Ace first touched down on the unit she was in bad shape. The jail or medical staff didn't give a fuck about her or her well-being because they put her in general population with two open wounds in her chest. The blessing behind the madness was that she was placed in Tammy's cell. Tammy helped Ace and nursed her back to health. She changed her bandages and made sure she got her jail ration of food that was issued out daily.

Tammy made sure she kept the other inmates off Ace's ass. When Ace was strong enough to walk to the phone, she called Ms. Cheryl and had Ms. Cheryl put two-thousand dollars on her account and five hundred dollars on Tammy's account. She also gave Ms. Cheryl the combo to her safe and informed her to hire a good attorney. Ms. Cheryl came through like a real mom would. She was so grateful she had Ms. Cheryl in her life. Ms. Cheryl had given her Musa's number. She'd been calling him twice a week and Musa had Skyped her.

Seeing Musa's handsome face gave her strength. Ace didn't even want to deal with her current situation from the encounter she had with her lawyer last month. There was overwhelming evidence that would put her in prison for the rest of her life. Despite all the incriminating evidence she had to take it to trial. The prosecutor wanted her to flip on Musa and say that Musa ordered the hit from jail to kill his parole officer. Ace would suck the devil's dick before she did some shit like that.

Musa encouraged her to keep fighting the case. He informed her that he was gonna put all his money behind her and on getting her free or less time as possible. Ace guessed that was the reason Musa hadn't had Brim killed for shooting her and betraying Money Mafia.

Musa needed Brim to continue to move the work. Due to Ace's phone calls and videos being recorded they hadn't spoke much about Brim. Musa did let her know he had gotten the message about Brim and what he did and with Ace knowing that she felt assured that Brim would get his soon or later.

"You cooking tonight, Tammy?" Ace asked.

"Yup if you take a bitch around the world with your pic and tell me some stories about how a boss bitch was living out there," Tammy replied.

"Fa sho', girl, but let me go down here and call mama Cheryl. I need a motherly talk today," Ace said walking out of the cell.

Tammy followed close behind like a well train pit bull.

Chapter 31

Musa sat on his bunk checking his stocks on his cell phone through his Robin Hood account. Tonight, the prison was quiet, maybe it was due to the storm that was taking place outside or the fact that everyone had something on their mind and rest couldn't come to them. Musa's thoughts turned to Shoota. He missed his partner, and he hated things turned out the way they did between them. The thought of his actions and selfishness toward Shoota was the lamest shit he had ever done. No matter if Shoota had gone his separate ways, he was still Money Mafia. In Musa's heart he would forever be.

He racked his brain behind who could have bought Shoota the move. The thought of Shoota's body lying in a shallow grave troubled his heart. It was unbelievable how things were on the up and up one second and the next, your closest friends were nonexistent or dead. The shit with Brim had him feeling like a sucka, but Musa knew he had to play chess, not checkers.

For now, he'd allow Brim to live and run the bag up. He had made up his mind he was out of the game once he stepped foot back on the other side. There was no reason to be in the game when the people who helped him start Money Mafia's movement was no longer part of his inner circle. Musa checked the time on his phone, it read 3:45 a.m. The guards made their rounds forty-five minutes ago. He had fifteen minutes before they made their next rounds.

Musa laid down on his bunk and laid the phone next to him. He closed his eyes and thought about Ace. He thought of her in an intimate way. He let his mind drift to the night of his birthday when they were in the back of the limo. Their kiss felt so right and engaged with passion and desire. Musa push his hand down the front of his sweats and felt his manhood swell. He thought about the softness of Ace's backside. He grew harder. That night he could see the love in Ace's eyes for him. That was another reason why he couldn't continue to deny her. He loved Ace just as much she loved him. Musa could hear the officer's keys clink as he walked down the tier to make his rounds. He removed his hand from his sweats. The officer's flashlight quickly lit his cell and quickly the light was gone.

Musa got up to put the phone away behind the brick carved out under his locker, but the phone vibrated in his hand. An unknown number appeared on the screen. Musa was hesitant to answer because there was only two people that had his number. His mom and Ace.

He hit the talk button, "Hello!" Musa whispered.

All he could hear on the other end of the phone was breathing.

"Who the fuck is this!" Musa spoke a little louder.

"Money Mafia all day every day!' A raspy voice came back through the phone.

"Shoota!" Musa said, jumping to his feet and rushing to the door window to make sure the guard was gone off his tier.

"You thought I was dead, Mu?"

"Man, man." Musa's eyes watered with salty tears. "Man, you alive?"

"Yeah, but it was your man that tried to place me in the dirt," Shoota said with anger in his voice.

"Who? Who slim?"

"That wetback muthafucka Papaya! He tried to have me bagged because he thought I was gonna be a problem for you, Musa. He thought I wanted to take over the operation. He was thinking I was going to snake you and by me doing that, it would fuck his money flow up."

The wheels in Musa's head started turning. He had conveyed to Papaya in the past of Shoota's bitterness and unhappiness. Papaya insisted that he put Shoota down and Musa was against it. Must thought harder. Since he'd been back in prison Papaya hadn't even mention Shoota's name. That could only be because he put the hit and also thought Shoota was died. Musa hadn't even mentioned to Papaya that Shoota got shot.

"How you know this, Shoota?"

"Well, I have a close business partner that is in the same line of work Papaya's in. They know some of the same people. Your name came up in an inquiry and it was revealed that Papaya had me popped because I wouldn't stay in line and be a good soldier. Musa, please tell me you wasn't in on it."

"What! Shoota don't fucking try me. I would never greenlight you. You my fucking brother, Shoota. I would give my last breath before I take yours," Musa confessed.

"Well, you may have to prove that you didn't have a hand in me getting popped. You been pillow talking to that nigga about me, Musa? There's no other way he knew we were having misunderstandings."

"How am I gonna prove that, Shoota? There is no way I can prove to you I wasn't with Papaya on the bullshit—"

"It is, Musa. It's always a way," Shoota stated firmly.

"How, Shoota? Tell me how," Musa begged.

"Kill his bitch ass!"

***

Shoota hung up the phone in Musa's ear. He poured himself a shot of Patron and blaze a blunt up. He had been lying up on a compound of the beach in Mexico. The night skies were full of stars. He could smell the ocean from where he sat. He owed it to Emma that he was still alive. The night after the club, she followed him and witnessed the shooting.

She had him pulled from the truck and he was rushed to one of her doctors that she had on payroll. The doc performed wonders on him. He removed three bullets from Shoota's body. Two from his back and one from his neck which left him talking kind of raspy. During recovery Shoota had Emma send some of her goons to Baltimore with a package and instructions for Bagz and Hell-Cat to keep things poppin'. Bagz and Hell-Cat had proven to be loyal to Shoota. Them niggas were getting it in in B-More and every dollar that belong to Shoota was sent back to him with a request to send more product.

Shoota had lost the ten bricks Musa gave him the night he got shot, but Emma's product proved to be more potent than what he was getting from Musa So, he struck a deal with Emma and she was now his new plug. Shoota could have been gone back to D.C. and Baltimore but he had the situation of Jassii being murdered in his truck to deal with and that he wasn't ready to face right now. He also had to deal with the dilemma of worrying if Papaya still had the contract on his head. He got word through Emma that Papaya thought he was dead. Shoota wasn't ready to test the waters to find out if Papaya really believed that.

Emma came clean with Shoota. She helped him because she wanted the whole East coast to be pushing her product. Papaya was her competition. She'd heard that Papaya was gonna make a play to take over the whole East coast and he was gonna use Musa to do it. When Emma found that out she did her homework on Musa and Money Mafia. She was gonna push up on Musa at his birthday party and make him an offer to leave Papaya and join her. If Musa would have refused that night, she already had her people in place to murder the whole Money Mafia when they walked out of the club. That was until, she saw Shoota and something in her made her change her tactics.

"Did you make the call, Shoota?" Emma asked, walking onto the balcony.

"Yeah, I did—" Shoota paused." I think he's gonna come through for us. I hope he does the right by me and our brotherhood."

Emma stepped in front of Shoota, removed the glass of Patron from his hand and took a sip. "Good, we got business to handle."

Chapter 32

Musa walked out of his cell the next morning feeling tired. His thoughts were consumed with last night's conversation with Shoota. Finding out Papaya had greenlighted Shoota had his nerves raw. He clenched his jaw muscles. Many inmates were getting ready for the morning meal. Musa wasn't a breakfast person in fact he never went to any of the prison meals. Everything that he ate was commissary bought. Or Papaya invited him to a meal that one of the guards had brought in for him. Musa wanted to hit the yard, do some pull ups, clear his mind and start the process of plotting Papaya's death. Musa made his way out of his unit into the corridor. The breakfast traffic was heavy going to the chow hall.

"Que paso, Amigo?" Papaya greeted Musa as he walked out his housing unit.

The sudden presence of Papaya was too sudden to hide the enmity he had scrolled across his face for Papaya.

Papaya immediately picked up on it. "What's the matter, Musa? You're looking at me like I've slept with your wife or killed your friend or something." Papaya searched Musa's eyes.

The killer in Musa's eyes slowly faded and it was a struggle to get them to soften and check his emotion. The man standing before him once told him, *"A man that moves on impulse is not a man but only a crash dummy and would rob himself of great opportunities to be victorious."*

"Naw, Papaya, it's nothing like that. The walls closing in on me this morning. Me spending most nights up, thinking about what I left out there in the streets and Ace got me wanting to go fuck shit up."

Papaya stared at Musa and a had hit of empathy. "Been there many times, mi Amigo, but channel that negative energy into something positive."

"I know that's why I'm about to hit the yard and do some pull ups and think. Hopefully, when I'm done, I will have a better perspective about where I'm at in life and my situation," Musa said as he and an older inmate that was walking past made eye contact, recognition reflected in both of their eyes but Musa couldn't remember where he knew the man from.

"Well, you do that, Musa. I will get with you later. I'm heading to the chow hall. There's something I need to discuss with the head of the Black Gorilla family," Papaya said, pushing forward through the crowded corridor with bodyguards trailing behind him.

Musa stared at the back of Papaya's head as his face broke down into a mug. Malice crept on Musa's face. Musa hit the rec yard, went straight to the pull up bar and started jerking up on the bar bringing his chin over the bar with every pull. He did twenty pull ups before he let go of the bar, dropped down and knocked off thirty push-ups. Musa came to his feet and was faced with the familiar face he saw in the corridor when he was talking to Papaya.

Musa was staring face to face with a skinny old timer with a sunken face and a pair of grey eyes. Musa looked at the old timer's hands checking for a weapon while still trying to remember where he encountered the man from.

"When I asked you to come see me, I wasn't speaking like this," the older man said spreading his arms in a manner to let Musa know he was referring to the prison.

"Man, you got me mistaken. I don't know you, O.G.!" Musa said watching the man intensely

"So, you don't recognize your own pops when you see him? Musa, it's me Moses your father."

Musa's chest became tight as he blinked his eyes open and shut. He couldn't believe that his father was standing before him. The man looked totally different from the last time he saw him. He had waist length dreads that so many Jamaicans were known for. Moses was always known to have a muscular structure. But the man standing in front of him looked frail and weak. The grey eyes told the truth that Moses was Musa's dad.

Musa didn't know if he wanted to swing on his pops or hug him. All those hard times without his dad came tumbling back. However, the power of missing his father overpowered his anger. Musa hugged his dad in a bear hug. His old man hugged him back with tears in his eyes. Musa's father felt like a bag of bones in his arms.

Musa knew then that his pops was sick, that must have been the reason why Moses had written that letter to him asking him to come to see him. Musa stepped out of his father's embrace.

Before Musa could ask his questions, Moses interrupted, "Come on, son, let's sit down. I have so much to tell you and not enough time to do so."

Musa and his dad found a spot on the bench where no one was occupying. Musa stared at his dad with great magnitude.

"I know you want to know why I never came back to you and your mom?" The shade of his grey eyes turn two shades darker. "I had a job to do the next day for a big score. I went on the lick. Shit went wrong, two muthafuckas died and I ended up with a life sentence. I never reached out because I was in prison for life. And there wasn't shit I could have done to help you and your mother from a prison cell. So, I did nothing. I felt like a failure and couldn't bring myself to reach out to you and tell you that I had failed and I was never coming home."

Musa felt like his pops wasn't keeping it 100 with him. He felt like his pop was making excuses. "If that's the case then why come back into me and my mother's life?" Musa asked.

He desperately wanted to know. All types of emotions ran through his head. His pops had just told him that he had life in prison, but a part of him really wanted to know why his father would even bother to contact him if he truly felt the way he felt about the situation.

"Son, I'm sick. I have cancer, and only a few months to live."

Pain and empathy flash across Musa's eyes and Moses brushed it off quickly as he saw it.

"Don't feel sorry for me, son. I have lived my life as I saw fit and on my own accord. We are all going to die one day so instead of running from it, sometimes we just have to embrace it," Moses stated firmly looking into his son's eyes. "Me dying is not important, spending the rest of my life in prison is not important. What's important is that you unite with your sibling."

Musa's face frowned. *"Sibling?"* Musa asked.

"Yeah, you have a sister—" Moses let out a sigh. "Remember that day I took you shopping, and I took you to the projects over Southeast where I had you wait in the truck?"

Musa remembered the day like it was yesterday. That was the last day he saw his father. "Yeah, pops I remember."

"I was going to introduce you to your sister that day, but when I went to see your sister, she and her mother conveyed to me that your sister was into girls at nine years. I refused to introduce you to your gay sister." Moses wiped tears from his eyes. "The little girl that came out and sat on the steps of the building that day, that was your sister. Her name is Ace."

To Be Continued…
Money Mafia 2
Coming Soon

Money Mafia

Lock Down Publications and Ca$h Presents assisted
publishing packages.

BASIC PACKAGE $499
Editing
Cover Design
Formatting

UPGRADED PACKAGE $800
Typing
Editing
Cover Design
Formatting

ADVANCE PACKAGE $1,200
Typing
Editing
Cover Design
Formatting
Copyright registration
Proofreading
Upload book to Amazon

LDP SUPREME PACKAGE $1,500
Typing
Editing
Cover Design
Formatting
Copyright registration
Proofreading
Set up Amazon account
Upload book to Amazon
Advertise on LDP Amazon and Facebook page

***Other services available upon request. Additional charges may apply

Lock Down Publications
P.O. Box 944
Stockbridge, GA 30281-9998
Phone # 470 303-9761

Submission Guideline

Submit the first three chapters of your completed manuscript to ldpsub-missions@gmail.com, subject line: Your book's title. The manuscript must be in a .doc file and sent as an attachment. Document should be in Times New Roman, double spaced and in size 12 font. Also, provide your synopsis and full contact information. If sending multiple submissions, they must each be in a separate email.

Have a story but no way to send it electronically? You can still submit to LDP/Ca$h Presents. Send in the first three chapters, written or typed, of your completed manuscript to:

LDP: Submissions Dept
Po Box 944
Stockbridge, Ga 30281

DO NOT send original manuscript. Must be a duplicate.

Provide your synopsis and a cover letter containing your full contact information.

Thanks for considering LDP and Ca$h Presents.

Jibril Williams

<u>NEW RELEASES</u>

MOB TIES 3 by SAYNOMORE
CONFESSIONS OF A GANGSTA by NICHOLAS LOCK
MURDA WAS THE CASE by ELIJAH R. FREEMAN
THE STREETS NEVER LET GO by ROBERT BAPTISTE
MOBBED UP 4 by KING RIO
AN UNFORESEEN LOVE 2 by MEESHA
KING OF THE TRENCHES by GHOST & TRANAY ADAMS
A DOPEBOY'S DREAM by ROMELL TUKES
MONEY MAFIA by JIBRIL WILLIAMS

Money Mafia

Coming Soon from Lock Down Publications/Ca$h Presents

BLOOD OF A BOSS **VI**

SHADOWS OF THE GAME II

TRAP BASTARD II

By **Askari**

LOYAL TO THE GAME **IV**

By **T.J. & Jelissa**

IF TRUE SAVAGE **VIII**

MIDNIGHT CARTEL IV

DOPE BOY MAGIC IV

CITY OF KINGZ III

NIGHTMARE ON SILENT AVE II

By **Chris Green**

BLAST FOR ME **III**

A SAVAGE DOPEBOY III

CUTTHROAT MAFIA III

DUFFLE BAG CARTEL VII

HEARTLESS GOON VI

By **Ghost**

A HUSTLER'S DECEIT III

KILL ZONE II

BAE BELONGS TO ME III

By **Aryanna**

COKE KINGS V

KING OF THE TRAP III

By **T.J. Edwards**

GORILLAZ IN THE BAY V

3X KRAZY III

De'Kari

KINGPIN KILLAZ IV

Jibril Williams

STREET KINGS III

PAID IN BLOOD III

CARTEL KILLAZ IV

DOPE GODS III

Hood Rich

SINS OF A HUSTLA II

ASAD

RICH $AVAGE II

By Troublesome

YAYO V

Bred In The Game 2

S. Allen

CREAM III

By Yolanda Moore

SON OF A DOPE FIEND III

HEAVEN GOT A GHETTO II

By Renta

LOYALTY AIN'T PROMISED III

By Keith Williams

I'M NOTHING WITHOUT HIS LOVE II

SINS OF A THUG II

TO THE THUG I LOVED BEFORE II

By Monet Dragun

QUIET MONEY IV

EXTENDED CLIP III

THUG LIFE IV

By **Trai'Quan**

THE STREETS MADE ME IV

By **Larry D. Wright**

IF YOU CROSS ME ONCE II

Money Mafia

By **Anthony Fields**

THE STREETS WILL NEVER CLOSE II

By **K'ajji**

HARD AND RUTHLESS III

THE BILLIONAIRE BENTLEYS II

Von Diesel

KILLA KOUNTY II

By **Khufu**

MONEY GAME II

By **Smoove Dolla**

A GANGSTA'S KARMA II

By **FLAME**

JACK BOYZ VERSUS DOPE BOYZ

A DOPEBOY'S DREAM III

By **Romell Tukes**

MOB TIES IV

By **SayNoMore**

MURDA WAS THE CASE II

Elijah R. Freeman

THE STREETS NEVER LET GO II

By **Robert Baptiste**

AN UNFORESEEN LOVE III

By **Meesha**

KING OF THE TRENCHES II

by **GHOST & TRANAY ADAMS**

MONEY MAFIA

By **Jibril Williams**

Available Now

Jibril Williams

RESTRAINING ORDER **I & II**

By **CA$H & Coffee**

LOVE KNOWS NO BOUNDARIES **I II & III**

By **Coffee**

RAISED AS A GOON I, II, III & IV

BRED BY THE SLUMS I, II, III

BLAST FOR ME I & II

ROTTEN TO THE CORE I II III

A BRONX TALE I, II, III

DUFFLE BAG CARTEL I II III IV V VI

HEARTLESS GOON I II III IV V

A SAVAGE DOPEBOY I II

DRUG LORDS I II III

CUTTHROAT MAFIA I II

KING OF THE TRENCHES

By **Ghost**

LAY IT DOWN **I & II**

LAST OF A DYING BREED I II

BLOOD STAINS OF A SHOTTA I & II III

By **Jamaica**

LOYAL TO THE GAME I II III

LIFE OF SIN I, II III

By **TJ & Jelissa**

BLOODY COMMAS I & II

SKI MASK CARTEL I II & III

KING OF NEW YORK I II,III IV V

RISE TO POWER I II III

COKE KINGS I II III IV

BORN HEARTLESS I II III IV

KING OF THE TRAP I II

196

Money Mafia

By **T.J. Edwards**
IF LOVING HIM IS WRONG…I & II
LOVE ME EVEN WHEN IT HURTS I II III
By **Jelissa**
WHEN THE STREETS CLAP BACK I & II III
THE HEART OF A SAVAGE I II III
MONEY MAFIA
By **Jibril Williams**
A DISTINGUISHED THUG STOLE MY HEART I II & III
LOVE SHOULDN'T HURT I II III IV
RENEGADE BOYS I II III IV
PAID IN KARMA I II III
SAVAGE STORMS I II
AN UNFORESEEN LOVE I II
By **Meesha**
A GANGSTER'S CODE I &, II III
A GANGSTER'S SYN I II III
THE SAVAGE LIFE I II III
CHAINED TO THE STREETS I II III
BLOOD ON THE MONEY I II III
By **J-Blunt**
PUSH IT TO THE LIMIT
By **Bre' Hayes**
BLOOD OF A BOSS **I, II, III, IV, V**
SHADOWS OF THE GAME
TRAP BASTARD
By **Askari**
THE STREETS BLEED MURDER **I, II & III**
THE HEART OF A GANGSTA I II& III
By **Jerry Jackson**

Jibril Williams

CUM FOR ME I II III IV V VI VII
An **LDP Erotica Collaboration**
BRIDE OF A HUSTLA **I II & II**
THE FETTI GIRLS **I, II& III**
CORRUPTED BY A GANGSTA I, II III, IV
BLINDED BY HIS LOVE
THE PRICE YOU PAY FOR LOVE I, II ,III
DOPE GIRL MAGIC I II III
By **Destiny Skai**
WHEN A GOOD GIRL GOES BAD
By **Adrienne**
THE COST OF LOYALTY I II III
By Kweli
A GANGSTER'S REVENGE **I II III & IV**
THE BOSS MAN'S DAUGHTERS I II III IV V
A SAVAGE LOVE **I & II**
BAE BELONGS TO ME I II
A HUSTLER'S DECEIT I, II, III
WHAT BAD BITCHES DO I, II, III
SOUL OF A MONSTER I II III
KILL ZONE
A DOPE BOY'S QUEEN I II III
By **Aryanna**
A KINGPIN'S AMBITON
A KINGPIN'S AMBITION **II**
I MURDER FOR THE DOUGH
By **Ambitious**
TRUE SAVAGE I II III IV V VI VII
DOPE BOY MAGIC I, II, III
MIDNIGHT CARTEL I II III

198

Money Mafia

CITY OF KINGZ I II

NIGHTMARE ON SILENT AVE

By **Chris Green**

A DOPEBOY'S PRAYER

By **Eddie "Wolf" Lee**

THE KING CARTEL **I, II & III**

By **Frank Gresham**

THESE NIGGAS AIN'T LOYAL **I, II & III**

By **Nikki Tee**

GANGSTA SHYT **I II &III**

By **CATO**

THE ULTIMATE BETRAYAL

By **Phoenix**

BOSS'N UP **I , II & III**

By **Royal Nicole**

I LOVE YOU TO DEATH

By **Destiny J**

I RIDE FOR MY HITTA

I STILL RIDE FOR MY HITTA

By **Misty Holt**

LOVE & CHASIN' PAPER

By **Qay Crockett**

TO DIE IN VAIN

SINS OF A HUSTLA

By **ASAD**

BROOKLYN HUSTLAZ

By **Boogsy Morina**

BROOKLYN ON LOCK I & II

By **Sonovia**

GANGSTA CITY

Jibril Williams

Money Mafia

MURDAROBER WAS THE CASE
Elijah R. Freeman
GOD BLESS THE TRAPPERS I, II, III
THESE SCANDALOUS STREETS I, II, III
FEAR MY GANGSTA I, II, III IV, V
THESE STREETS DON'T LOVE NOBODY I, II
BURY ME A G I, II, III, IV, V
A GANGSTA'S EMPIRE I, II, III, IV
THE DOPEMAN'S BODYGAURD I II
THE REALEST KILLAZ I II III
THE LAST OF THE OGS I II III
Tranay Adams
THE STREETS ARE CALLING
Duquie Wilson
MARRIED TO A BOSS I II III
By Destiny Skai & Chris Green
KINGZ OF THE GAME I II III IV V
Playa Ray
SLAUGHTER GANG I II III
RUTHLESS HEART I II III
By Willie Slaughter
FUK SHYT
By Blakk Diamond
DON'T F#CK WITH MY HEART I II
By Linnea
ADDICTED TO THE DRAMA I II III
IN THE ARM OF HIS BOSS II
By Jamila
YAYO I II III IV
A SHOOTER'S AMBITION I II

Jibril Williams

BRED IN THE GAME
By S. Allen
TRAP GOD I II III
RICH $AVAGE
By Troublesome
FOREVER GANGSTA
GLOCKS ON SATIN SHEETS I II
By Adrian Dulan
TOE TAGZ I II III
LEVELS TO THIS SHYT I II
By Ah'Million
KINGPIN DREAMS I II III
By Paper Boi Rari
CONFESSIONS OF A GANGSTA I II III IV
By Nicholas Lock
I'M NOTHING WITHOUT HIS LOVE
SINS OF A THUG
TO THE THUG I LOVED BEFORE
By Monet Dragun
CAUGHT UP IN THE LIFE I II III
THE STREETS NEVER LET GO
By Robert Baptiste
NEW TO THE GAME I II III
MONEY, MURDER & MEMORIES I II III
By **Malik D. Rice**
LIFE OF A SAVAGE I II III
A GANGSTA'S QUR'AN I II III
MURDA SEASON I II III
GANGLAND CARTEL I II III
CHI'RAQ GANGSTAS I II III

Money Mafia

KILLERS ON ELM STREET I II III

JACK BOYZ N DA BRONX I II III

A DOPEBOY'S DREAM I II

By **Romell Tukes**

LOYALTY AIN'T PROMISED I II

By Keith Williams

QUIET MONEY I II III

THUG LIFE I II III

EXTENDED CLIP I II

By **Trai'Quan**

THE STREETS MADE ME I II III

By **Larry D. Wright**

THE ULTIMATE SACRIFICE I, II, III, IV, V, VI

KHADIFI

IF YOU CROSS ME ONCE

ANGEL I II

IN THE BLINK OF AN EYE

By **Anthony Fields**

THE LIFE OF A HOOD STAR

By Ca$h & Rashia Wilson

THE STREETS WILL NEVER CLOSE

By K'ajji

CREAM I II

By Yolanda Moore

NIGHTMARES OF A HUSTLA I II III

By King Dream

CONCRETE KILLA I II

By Kingpen

HARD AND RUTHLESS I II

MOB TOWN 251

Jibril Williams

THE BILLIONAIRE BENTLEYS
By Von Diesel
GHOST MOB
Stilloan Robinson
MOB TIES I II III
By SayNoMore
BODYMORE MURDERLAND I II III
By Delmont Player
FOR THE LOVE OF A BOSS
By C. D. Blue
MOBBED UP I II III IV
By King Rio
KILLA KOUNTY
By Khufu
MONEY GAME
By Smoove Dolla
A GANGSTA'S KARMA
By FLAME
KING OF THE TRENCHES II
by **GHOST & TRANAY ADAMS**

Money Mafia

BOOKS BY LDP'S CEO, CA$H

TRUST IN NO MAN

TRUST IN NO MAN 2

TRUST IN NO MAN 3

BONDED BY BLOOD

SHORTY GOT A THUG

THUGS CRY

THUGS CRY 2

THUGS CRY 3

TRUST NO BITCH

TRUST NO BITCH 2

TRUST NO BITCH 3

TIL MY CASKET DROPS

RESTRAINING ORDER

RESTRAINING ORDER 2

IN LOVE WITH A CONVICT

LIFE OF A HOOD STAR

Jibril Williams

CPSIA information can be obtained
at www.ICGtesting.com
Printed in the USA
BVHW041156070222
628298BV00012B/337